MW01240784

1

DERANGED MINDS

MINDS

R.C. RUMPLE

&

CHARLES LYNNE

This book is a work of fiction. References to real people, events, establishments, organizations, or locales are intended only to provide a sense of authenticity, and are used fictitiously. All other characters, and all incidents and dialogue, are drawn from the author's imagination and are not to be construed as real.

PUBLISHER'S NOTES

Thank You

R.C. Rumple – First, I need to give tremendous thanks to **Charles Lynne** for approaching me months ago and asking me if I'd like to be a part of this project. Charles had many ideas he had made attempts to develop into stories. I looked over what he had and saw extraordinary promise. They were darker than most of what I had ever personally written, and the idea of pursuing this avenue intrigued me. Thus, we began our efforts, much like Elton John and Bernie Taupin, each having our roles. He would supply the ideas, and I would transform them into stories to hold the reader's interest. Along the way, I developed a different style to my writing and began to create ideas of my own, still in this line of horror, which have also been added to this collection. In addition, the quality of writing we both demanded made me work harder than ever before. Charles, to you I am eternally grateful. Because of this co-authorship, I have developed both as a much better writer and as a creator of dark stories. Without Charles and the ideas and critical input he provided, this book would never have taken place. He earned his co-authorship equal credit status many times over. He is a valuable source of ideas, and a strong critic who demands perfection.

I also wish to thank **Becky Narron** for all her assistance along the way, as well as for the fantastic covers and foreword. My princess, you are too good to be true and your heart is bigger than the night sky cradling the moon. Your never-ending efforts to see this through to the end are appreciated more than you'll ever realize. My never-ending gratitude to you.

Tamra Crow, you did a great job of editing. We expected a lot and you didn't let us down. Fantastic job!

Charles Lynne - I'm usually better at writing pain, torture, and death than I am writing thank you's and praise. That said, this book would not be possible without the persistence, imagery, and the ability of **Richard Rumple** to take a few deranged ideas and turn them into a fully immersible story for the reader to get lost in. His ability to transform tell into show is something I continually strike out with, while he makes it seem like second nature. Thank you, Richard.

I also have to thank my sister, **Becky Narron**, for forcing me to put pen to paper, the stories I've told for years around campfires. Always in an attempt to keep everyone awake in the woods, worrying about every single rustle in the leaves, or random acorn that would bounce off the side of the tent. If not for Becky, my stories would simply be spoken, and never written. Thank you, Becky.

Most people do this, as well I. I need to thank my parents for, while being strict, always supporting any endeavor I pursued. Thank you, **Mom and Dad**.

Lastly, but certainly not least, I have to thank **Sadie Whitecoat**. She has reminded me that you should do your own thing, the way you want to, and never change who you are at your core for the convenience of others. Also, never be hesitant to tell your story, no matter what others may think. The poems she writes may be brutal at times, but life can be brutal, and she makes you want to view that brutality from her point of view. Thank you, Sadie.

Foreword

Writing a foreword for a book is an honor, and one I don't take lightly. So, before I forget, "Thank you" for asking me and giving me the honor.

Collections come in all different shapes and sizes. Some are just one author's works, others are two authors or three. This one is between the creative minds of Richard C. Rumple and Charles Lynne. The stories are diverse and will leave you wanting more. Some of the stories started from the mind of Charles Lynne, with Richard C. Rumple coming in and adding the flow and scenery. Others are a combination of both authors. Still others started with Richard C. Rumple, and had Charles Lynne's added touch. They are full of rich characters and great ambiance. You will be able to feel, taste, and almost touch what you are reading. You will remember them for years to come. They will haunt your mind, and make you look over your shoulder when you are walking in the dark. They will become favorites to read, over and over again.

I can tell you that this is one book I want a signed copy of for my collection. There are many reasons for this. Yes, one would be my writing the foreword. Another would be because the stories are solid and very well-written. I know these guys have worked very hard on this, and spent many hours making sure the stories were perfect, so that people would be able to relate to them and that you could feel the fear the characters felt. Nothing in this world is ever perfect, but I will say this book is pretty damn close. So, enjoy your read from the two Deranged Minds that make up this collection. I wish you good luck and good journey. Most importantly, remember to tell your friends, and leave a review.

Becky Narron

Table of Contents

The Back Seat

Urban legends ... the stuff we laugh at, right?

How many movies have we seen, books have we read, and stories have we heard? Lovers Lane cars with a hook dangling from the door handle, razor blades in Halloween candy, or even strangers hiding in the backseats of cars ... all legends without proof. These are the tales told to children to scare them, to make them follow rules, to help them understand there is evil in this world and to be wary. Of course, kids see their parents ignoring these very rules. When was the last time you saw your parents look in the backseat before entering a car? Doesn't set a very good example, does it?

I was no different than anyone else. As I grew up, I challenged what they'd said, and ignored their warnings. I made out with my boyfriends in the most deserted of country locations, munched Halloween candy before inspecting it, and can't ever remember looking in the backseat of my car before entering. I wasn't reckless or foolhardy, I simply didn't take their warnings as necessary. I was smart enough not to do the most stupid of things, like walk in a high crime area after midnight, or jump in a stranger's van to give directions. The people that do are the same who believe blankets are magic and will keep monsters away. Some people are idiots and will get themselves in trouble, no matter what. It's inevitable.

The only thing those tales ever did for me was to spice up the night. You know, make the imagination run wild. They made you feel alive, while fearing death and torture. It was nice while it lasted. But you get older and get a boring job, and then nothing is exciting. Many, like myself, drudge away our lives in one of the few factories remaining in the country. We go to work, slave like mindless zombies for eight hours (sometimes twelve if overtime is available), end up exhausted, and go home to our mundane existence and families. The high point of the evening is going to bed knowing you'll get to do it all over again the next day. Oh, what fun, what fun!

Today began the same as always. I got to work, started up my press, and began banging out metal strips for conductor plates. About an hour in, the foreman gathered us off to the side and gave us the news. Seemed the company was way behind on a contract, and up against a wall. The product had to be produced and shipped by midnight, no exceptions. We were asked to work four hours of overtime, and then four additional hours. If we completed the order, we would make double time, not just for the extra four, but for the entire overtime. But, if we didn't make the order deadline, the head office was going to close the doors to the factory … for good.

There's always a hitch to good news, isn't there?

The words about closing the factory for good had a major impact. None of us working did so for fun, we needed the money. None of us could afford to be unemployed. I was the only breadwinner in my family, and had to bring home the bucks. My husband's factory had already closed and left him unemployed. I couldn't lose my job, too. China factory labor costs were a real threat, not one only used to get us motivated.

Most of us agreed to the extra hours. There were a few who sloughed off the threat, and a couple of single mothers who didn't have anyone to care for their children, but the majority stayed. We vowed to keep the doors open, and our incomes safe. We had no option.

The day passed slower than any I'd ever put in. I finished my final plate ten minutes before the deadline. Reaching up, I hit the OFF button. Nothing happened. I hit it again ... and again ... until the machine finally shut down. I'd complained about the short in it before. When I got back tomorrow morning, it would be justice if it didn't start.

I headed to the break room and sat down. My back and arms ached almost as much as my feet. Too many hours, and not enough break times. All I wanted was to clock out, get home, and soak my body in a hot tub for a few minutes. I wouldn't have time to soak for long, though. It was almost midnight. I was due back, and ready to put in another day's work, in seven hours. Yeah, the fun just kept coming.

The buzzer sounded, ending our shift. An announcement was made over the intercom that we'd made the deadline. I expected to hear cheers, but there were none. Everyone must have been too tired. I headed to the locker room to change clothes and head home. It was strange. The room was empty, except for me. I figured there were other women down the line who would be there, but none showed. It was so eerie to be there all alone. I trembled as a cold chill ran through me. Rubbing my hands up and down my bare arms, I did my best to run away the goosebumps. Turning to leave, I slammed the door of my locker—the metal upon metal echoing ominously. Hopefully, it had scared away any lingering goblins.

Outside, the cool of the late September night helped to revive me. The lot was almost empty, which explained the empty locker room. I guessed most had said the hell with it and worn their work clothes home, instead of changing. If I'd have been smart, I probably would have done the same. Tomorrow would be interesting, though, as they'd be trying to sneak them back inside, past the morning guards.

I stopped and did a quick turnaround, as I didn't remember seeing a guard at the shack on the way out. The light was on, but no guard was inside. Odd, there was always supposed to be someone there to open the gates, for late night deliveries and such. Figuring he was taking a bathroom break, I turned and headed to my car.

That morning, the lot had been almost full. Large enough to handle the needs of its employees, it was well over the length of a football field, and I'd parked only a few spaces from the end. Many of the lot lights had burnt out and not been replaced, while others buzzed and created a strobe effect. Being a woman, alone, in a dark lot was scary enough, but with the on-and-off lighting, my imagination began playing tricks on me. My mind recalled the days of my youth, when Dad would force me to watch monster movies with him. I hated them then, and I still do—just not my thing. Give me a happy movie where everyone lives, and no throats are slashed, any day.

"Watch this, JoAnne," he'd whisper, thinking he would trick me into opening my eyes for a scary part. "Look, look, open your eyes. You're missing the good part."

Yeah, he was a sadistic bastard.

He got so mad when I wouldn't comply. Not only did he tease me for being a sissy, he'd send me to bed. Little did he know, that was my plan. There, I could hide under the magic covers and be safe from the monsters.

The rustling of dried leaves and cardboard pieces drew my attention back to the parking lot. There was something dark moving off to my left. I focused, trying to distinguish the shape hugging the ground. The best I could tell, it looked like a giant rat. I shuddered at the thought. It moved again, first to my front and then straight at me. A lot light flickered. In the strobe, an opossum appeared. We stared at each other, both petrified, until it decided to make a break toward the open field, just outside the flimsy fence the company called employee security. (We joked about it during storms, wondering what member of maintenance we'd hear cussing about having to go put it back up.)

Taking a deep breath, I gathered myself. My car was still fifty yards away, somewhere in the dark ahead. My imagination working overtime, I stood, trying to decide upon a route to get to it that would take me away from the couple of vehicles remaining in the lot. Why chance running into a maniac lurking behind one?

Okay, so I was letting the midnight hour affect my way of thinking. I realized that, but was still nervous. The flickering and buzzing of lights, the dark spots in the lot, being alone—I had a right to be wary. I hurried my pace, each step sounding louder than the last, and echoing in the emptiness surrounding me. I stopped. Thinking I'd heard footsteps behind me, I turned. Nothing was there. The hairs on my arms stood up, as if to send out radar beams to alert me of an unknown presence. Nothing. Deafened by the silence, I moved on.

In the shadows, my car appeared—my den of safety. I giggled. *Yeah, den of safety, you'd better start. I'm in no mood to sit here waiting for a wrecker.* I opened the door and tossed in my lunchbox as I sat down. Shadows of demon-like hands reached out of the darkness and sent me tumbling back out of the door and down to the unforgiving pavement. I scrambled to escape, hesitating only to turn and catch a glimpse of what could be inside. Nothing, nothing at all.

My intuition screamed, "Flee! Head back to the lights of the factory!" Yet, I remained. There was nothing there, nothing to be afraid of, nothing to keep me from going home but my own imagination. With caution, I walked around the car, looking inside to ensure I was alone. No one in front, no one in back—the car was empty. I was happy no one was there to witness my paranoia. Unexplainably, I still felt as though I wasn't alone. The open driver's door showed no one in the front. So, they had to be hiding in the backseat. They had to! Not in the seat itself, but across the car, in the floorboard. I needed to see, even though it meant putting myself in tremendous danger. I had to know what was there. I grabbed hold of the handle and yanked, sending the door flying open.

Nothing.

This was crazy. There had to be someone in the car. I didn't imagine the hands reaching for me. Somewhere, they had to be hiding, but where? Then it hit me, they had been in the backseat, but had pulled down the seat and rolled into the trunk! That was it, it had to be. They were back there, waiting for me to take off, all distraught, and when we got out on the road, they would make their attack. I'd be a helpless victim, and they'd show no mercy. I'd be dead, and there would be no witnesses nor cameras to know who did it.

I convinced myself they were there and developed a plan, a plan that would ruin theirs. I'd open the trunk and expose them. They had to know there were cameras, as well as a security guard, on the premises. Surely, they wouldn't attack me here. No, I'd open the trunk, and they'd run like a scared little schoolyard bully.

Reaching under the front dash, I pulled the trunk release lever. The thud of the lid being released vibrated through my body. Walking to the back, I slid my fingers under the cool metal and flipped it up, hard. I jumped back, in case my foe hadn't listened to my thoughts of logic and leapt out to attack.

Nothing. Not a damn thing.

This was ridiculous. I had listened to my imagination and made it sound logical. I'd probably sat down in the front seat, dropped off immediately to sleep, and had a nightmare. All my fears, and searching for a maniac or a monster of sorts, had been the result. I chuckled, "JoAnne, if your father could see you now. He'd probably be rolling on the floor and laughing his ass off. You're one brave girl, you are, one brave girl … not. Shut the damn trunk lid and backdoor, and drive yourself home before you give yourself a heart attack."

After shutting all the doors, I climbed back in and hit the lock button. I was surrounded by the thuds and clicks of each door securing itself. Nothing inside, and no way to get in, I rested my head against the steering wheel and whispered a "Thank you" to the man upstairs. Sitting tall, I took a deep breath and drove toward the gate.

The rumbling of a menacing growl came from behind me.

Slamming on the brakes, I jammed the car into Park and frantically exited, falling to the pavement and crawling away as fast as I could. My knees dispatched their declarations of pain from the fragments of a broken beer bottle that sliced deep, and I rolled to my back, ready to kick and claw any attacker.

But none came. Only the constant buzzing from the lights was present.

I broke down and let the tears flow. This was too much. I was exhausted. If this is what it felt to have a mental breakdown, I was having one. Sitting up, I pulled a shard of the beer bottle from my knee, and then another. I didn't feel the pain of their extractions, only the gentle flow of the blood as it left my body.

Nerves spent, I struggled to my feet and got back in the car. If the creature wanted me, it could have me. I had no more strength to fight it off. Courage had given way to fear, yet even that was gone, for the moment. I began to wonder if the parking lot was haunted and never wanted me to leave. I visualized my co-workers arriving in the morning and finding me sitting there, claiming the parking lot was holding me hostage. I'd be transported away to a hospital, lose my job, allow my family to starve and become homeless.

I couldn't let that happen. I had to take control.

Shifting the car into Drive, I moved forward. I refused to hear, and refused to fear. If it had been able to harm me, it already would have done so. It was bluffing and I would prove it. I slowed for the guard shack,` but found it still empty. Punching the accelerator, I pulled onto the highway and into the darkness.

A weak buzzing sound began from the backseat. I laughed and dared it to do something, knowing the further I got away from its home, the less strength it would have. I used an old trick I'd used many times as a teenager. If you don't want to hear the car's noises, turn on the radio!

Commercials filled my ears. No longer would the buzzing bother me. The sound of wonderful radio commercials had taken its place. I couldn't wait on the commercial break to be done. I needed music. Switching the channel, I found more commercials. Another channel change, and more commercials. Channel after channel and no change. It was as if the world of FM radio was in a non-stop loop of commercial breaks. Switching to the AM mode, I found a news station. Not my favorite, but better than commercials. After a few minutes, the radio stopped working and only a buzzing came through the speakers. Turning it off, I drove in silence.

Passing familiar signs, I noticed the stoplight was out at the intersection ahead. I stopped, looked both ways, and slowly proceeded through, fearing a police officer was hiding off to the side for traffic offenders. Last thing I needed was a ticket. I kept to the speed limit as I began passing the wildlife preserve area. Such a beautiful drive during the day, the night brought only the ominous shadows of darkness. Tree limbs reached out to the cars speeding by on the highway, barely escaping their grasp. I tapped the accelerator to get through the preserve faster, no longer worried about meeting oncoming traffic, or the police. If they hadn't been back at the intersection, they'd be hanging out around the late-night bars, in hopes of catching drunk drivers. Still on edge, I sat back in the seat and forced myself to try to relax.

Suddenly, a damn deer jumped onto the highway. The son-of-a-bitch didn't keep going. It just stopped and watched as I slammed on the brakes, so hard I nearly drove my brake pedal through the floor. The front of the car nosedived, fought my control, and my purse and lunchbox shot forward and rammed against the dash. Something hit the back of my seat, but I didn't have time to worry about it. Clutching the steering wheel with all my strength, I skidded to a stop, only a few feet from the animal. I turned and gave a quick check of the backseat. I'd felt the force of something hitting the seat, but knew I'd find nothing. I was right. Whatever had been there was gone. I'd expected no less.

Settling back, I noticed the eyes of the deer reflected a green glow in the headlight beams. It had not been there at first, but was evident now. The glow surged forward, piercing my brain with sparks and a deafening buzzing. I was on fire. In seconds I would turn to ashes. I screamed!

Then, nothing. The pain vanished.

I opened my eyes to a normal deer standing in front of my car. There were no glowing eyes. Those had disappeared. Now, the simple creature's eyes only reflected my car's headlights. The deer seemed to stare at me, almost daring me to move forward, to attempt to force it from its position. I honked the horn, in hopes of startling it. Instead, the animal raised its antler heavy head and opened its mouth, as if returning my challenge. The stalemate lasted another minute ... and then two. Deciding itself victorious, the deer stepped from the road and out of the headlight beams, and disappeared into the darkness. The road ahead was empty, no obstacles remained. Gradually, I let the car begin to roll. Getting a grip on myself, I sped up. I did hope to be home before daybreak.

I wondered about my companion in the backseat. *When would he reappear? Why was he being so silent? What was the reason he remained? Had he grown so weakened by the distance from the factory, he could do nothing? What would happen when I went back to work tomorrow? Had I gained a constant companion, or would he seek out another, more amiable to his desires? If it was me he wanted, what did I have to offer, my soul? What did he need to do to collect it?*

At least thinking about whatever it was back there kept my mind active. He could linger all he wanted, as long as he stayed in the car when I got home. I no longer had any doubt of his presence. I just couldn't see him. There was no comfort in that fact—simply fear.

The streetlights of the city, a couple of miles up the road, normally lit up the night. Tonight, even they seemed to be out of order. It was as if the area had suffered a power outage. They'd lost a substation due to a traffic accident or some other reason, before, but this was something much greater. I needed to get home and make sure my family was safe. I pushed the speed a little faster, knowing the sooner I could pull into my driveway and escape from this nightmare, the better.

Less than a mile and a half to go, my headlights went dark and my engine stopped. I was still moving, but not able to see where I was going. I turned the wheel to the right, to leave the pavement, but it had no effect. Again, pulling with all my might and weight, I turned the wheel. Still, the pavement of the highway lay underneath my wheels. The car had rolled to a stop sitting in the middle of the lane. I tried turning on my emergency flashers but, like everything else, they were dead.

I was caught between tears and anger. The night had not been kind. This was the icing on the cake.

Behind me, the scraping of claws raked across the back of my seat. The demon had awakened.

I looked into my rearview mirror to catch a glance of what was to cause my death. Two white lights glowed back at me. There was no reason to flee. The tenacity it had exhibited in staying with me was beyond my means to escape. "If you're going to kill me, let's get the damn thing over with!" I screamed at the reflection. "I'm going to fight you, that you can bet on. I don't give up easy—never have and never will. Bring your best, you bastard!"

The lights grew brighter and larger. I waited to feel my attacker's hot breath against my neck. I had pulled the keys from the ignition and planned to jab them in his eyes at the first opportunity. If I could blind him, I might be able to escape in the darkness. I readied myself for his attack. I needed him to make the first move. Only then could I catch him by surprise.

The eyes in the mirror bounced a little, and swayed left and right. What in the hell had I been thinking? There wasn't a beast behind me. It was a car, coming up fast. With no flashers, it would never see me in time. A crash was imminent.

I leapt from my car, waving my arms in hopes they'd see me. I didn't want an innocent family to die because of me or my old rattletrap. A quick prayer rolled off my lips. Closer and closer, it hadn't slowed at all. I screamed, a useless act, but I needed to do something to save them, and it was all I could do. It was too little, too late. The oncoming vehicle reached the rear of mine. I jumped away, hoping to avoid being caught by the flying debris. But there was no crash.

As if in slow-motion, the car melted into mine and traveled through it … as if it wasn't there. Three pairs of eyes, glowing as those of the deer had done, stared my direction as they passed by. It was over in a matter of seconds. Flabbergasted, I watched the taillights of the other vehicle drive off into the night.

From inside my car, I heard my phone ringing. So much had happened, I'd forgotten I even had one.
I ran to grab it, but the ringing ceased before I could answer. The call showed no number. Again, it rang. I hit

the answer button, yet no one was there. The text alert sounded. It was from my husband.

"Are you coming home tonight?" he asked.

"I wish I knew," I whispered to myself. Before I could respond to his question, the phone died. I guess it wasn't used to working sixteen-hour days, either.

Then, my car's headlights came on and the engine started, without the key. The dashboard lights provided enough illumination to see the driver's seat was empty. The beast was luring me back. I shook my head in disbelief and the engine revved up. I had no choice. I was being ordered back.

Once in the driver's seat, the car slipped itself into gear and began to move. I reached for the wheel but found it was being controlled. I sat, hands in lap, waiting to see where I ended up being taken.

Pulling into my driveway, mixed emotions surfaced. I was home, my safe place, the residence of my family. My kids were inside, asleep by now, hopefully having wonderful dreams of pink animals and sunshiny days. It was my responsibility to provide them love and protection.

Yet, I had not been able to protect myself this evening. I'd brought a demon home with me, an evil one, to invade their safe world, a creature who could do them harm. It hadn't been planned. I'd done my best to keep it from happening. I'd even told it to take me. But it was here, in this car, at my house.

I saw the red glow of a cigarette being smoked over to my left, just beyond the front door. The face of my husband shone in the dim light. My first thoughts were to scold him. He had quit four months back. Then, I wondered what could have made him pick them back up again? And, why hadn't he come over to the car when I pulled in? Was he upset I hadn't been able to respond to his text?

Reaching for the door handle, my fingers fell short of their grasp. Thinking I was just super-tired, I tried again and was shocked to see them pass through the handle, as if it was air. A gripping force rushed through my body, a charge that arched my body to the sky. The buzzing of electricity gone wild invaded my skull through my ears, and couldn't find an exit. My brain boiled and mouth foamed, the nerve synapses refusing to cooperate, to allow me to fight. Voices, screaming in the background, came through the static, the buzz, demanding action. I felt my hand smoking, blackened by whatever the energy had been that had taken me on this journey into pain, but dropped me off in the land of eternal numbness. Another light was calling me. My family would have to wait. Again, I was being controlled. I had a feeling this would be the last time.

* * * * *

"Man, this sucked. She was an all right lady. Never complained, always on time, a good person all around. So, do you think the husband will sue the company?"

26

"He'd be a fool not to. I understand she'd been reporting that button had a short in it for months. Shame a person had to die because no one gave a damn. But, if that's the way the company wants to do it, let them pay the price. I understand they're moving to China, anyway. Fuck 'em."

Buzzing Flies

The living room carpet is soaked red around my wife's ravaged torso. Ragged strips of flesh dangle from the gashes and brush against the bloodstains forming in the piles of the thick tan fabric. Stray bits of partially-eaten vital organs draw a mass of houseflies, previously absent from the home's interior. Their origin is a mystery, but there is no relief from the droning that interrupts the otherwise silent scene.

I fall to my knees, sobbing, my guts ripping apart, seeming to duplicate the pain she felt in her last moments. Before me, my love, the foundation of my existence, the mother of my children, gone forever. I exhale and lean my forehead to the floor, inches from the blood, no longer expanding from its host. My mind demands the tears and gasping cease. There will be time for grief later. I must find our young ones, elsewhere in the house. I listen for any hint of where they may be. There is only the buzzing of the flies.

I fear the kids have met the same fate as my wife, but am too distraught to rise. The fear and apprehension of seeing them lying ripped to shreds, drains all energy. I should be frantic, rushing to their aid. Yet, I have little to no hope. The tears are not returning—the shock of what I've seen prevents the ducts from releasing them.

The warmth of our home, and the love we shared, is gone, absent from my inner soul. I am empty, neither sad nor happy—only a shell, existing for no viable reason.

28

My efforts to raise a family, and see a future built, have been eradicated in violence. There will be no college graduations to bring joy, no weddings to give my daughters away, no grandchildren on my knees—the plans, all for naught. I am alone.

Forcing myself to get to my feet, I compel myself to seek out the bodies of my children. The first floor holds only that of my wife, the basement is empty. I trudge up the stairs, each step heavier than the last, not wanting to find the end of my dreams. I hear the laughter of playing in their room, but find it departs with my next step. My hopes are playing games in my mind. Shaking my head, my efforts to dispel fiction and accept reality meet, with a battle between the fantasy of hope, and the disappointment of what is expected to be found.

The upstairs bathroom door is partially closed, as are all the doors on this level. It is odd. My wife always insisted on the doors being fully opened, to allow the sunlight to shine in and the air to circulate. She would have had a fit seeing them this way. This has been done purposely, hoping to either upset her while she lived, or to frustrate her spirit in death.

I push back the bathroom door and find the room empty. I repeat this at our bedroom door and find the same. There are two doors left—the guest room, and the bedroom assigned to the girls. I save the anticipated horror for last and give the guest room door a shove. It, too, is empty.

Standing in front of the final door, I hesitate, taking a deep breath, in hopes to prepare myself for the grim scene lying behind the wooden barrier. Visions, too horrible to imagine, force their way in, scoffing at my self-imposed mental restrictions. My tears have broken through the dam and blur all before me. Their wish, only to provide some mercy from the horror that lies beyond. Yet, I must witness the horror with the clarity needed to never forget—to be able to speak with knowledge as the attorney questions what I found, when the guilty party is charged. I wipe them away with my sleeves.

The door swings open at the touch of my fingers. Lying on the bed are my girls. They seem to be unharmed—sleeping soundly—with my wife napping between them!

I stop breathing. My muscles lock. I blink several times. Am I imagining what is before my eyes? There lies my family—unharmed and alive. How can this be? My wife lies downstairs, savagely attacked, her body ravaged and shredded. I cannot look away. Fear of losing what's before me is too great. What if I turn away and then turn back, only to find the children there? Or, what if I turn back and the children are ripped apart, as my wife has been? Confusion reigns supreme and my sanity seeks to locate itself. Yet, I have no option—I must chance it.

I close my eyes and tilt my head to the floor. Silently counting to ten, I open my eyes and raise my head. The scene has changed, as I feared it might. My wife has disappeared. One of the girls is sitting on the side of the bed, her back to me. The other is lying still, a pillow over her face. Her chest is motionless, no sign of breathing taking place. I move forward to see if she is alive, or if she has joined her mother in death. A fierce growl rumbles from her sister—a warning to stop in my tracks. I turn, shaken by the changing visions and sounds, not knowing what is real. I step on some toy—a boobytrap placed to inhibit those trespassing—and lose my balance. Stumbling ahead, I reach for the door frame, in hopes of maintaining my upright position. Something is pushing me down, wanting me to fall, to become easier prey. The growling is above me. I struggle to scramble from danger, from death. A heavy weight keeps me down, making escape impossible. Claws rip into my shoulders, and strong jaws clamp onto the back of my head. There is a cracking, a popping, as bone gives way to the pressure and my skull is crushed. My scream is cut short as blackness overcomes me. I know I am dead.

"What's wrong with Daddy?"

It is a voice almost identical to my oldest daughter's. My gut tells me it is not her, but one wanting to deceive. I'm guessing there is only one present here, besides myself. It is speaking as if another is present, in hopes I will open my eyes. I will not grant its wish.

I'm surprised to be alive. I was being killed only moments before. There is little pain, only a headache throbbing through my temple. Whatever I'm reclining on is soft, soft like my bed would be. I wonder how I got here, who put me here, and what is waiting for me when I open my eyes? A cool, damp cloth gently runs across my forehead and dabs at my eyes and cheeks. It is refreshing, and makes me wish to see who holds it. Yet, I'm afraid ... afraid it may only be a ruse to trick me into opening my eyes. I feign unconsciousness, praying it will tire and walk away—and I might then see what leaves, saving me for future torture.

I am being toyed with—a victim of some creature's sadistic amusement. Anger grows within, wanting to slash out and destroy my puppet master. Fear restrains me, frustrates me, denies me. Should I show any semblance of being even semi-conscious, I know it would leap at the chance to inflict more pain and punishment. There is no desire inside of me for this to occur. I lie still.

"Your father isn't well," a voice like my wife's responds. "He fell and hit his head against the door frame. If he doesn't come to soon, we need to call the doctor and maybe an ambulance. I'd have already done it, if money wasn't so tight right now. Where's your sister at? Go find her."

There is a child's exasperated exhale and the sound of tiny tennis shoes scrunching against the hardwood floor, leaving the room. Surely, if there was only one of the creatures present, I would be alone, free to open my eyes and examine my surroundings. But, what would I see?

32

Since arriving home, I'd seen my wife's bloody body lying dead on the living room floor, my wife and girls napping, one daughter dead, and the other one becoming a beast of some sort. I had entered a world of ever-changing reality and fiction, much like the imagination of a deranged madman, unable to decide what direction to roam. My world, normally so sane and boring, had become a universe of horrendous alternatives. I had no answers. Lost in a mass of confusion, logic made no sense. There was no action creating a reaction, only visions and nightmares. I had left a completely average family in the morning, and returned home to a world of horror.

Maniacal laughter sounded from outside the room, possibly from downstairs. I chanced discovery and peeked. I was in my bedroom, alone and safe, for the time being. I chuckled at "safe", knowing that it was only relative to the moment. From what I had witnessed tonight, our home had become an asylum for demons and spirits.

Sliding as softly as possible to my feet, I hurried to the dresser and opened the top drawer. From below a stack of my underwear, I removed a case and entered the combination into the lock. Opening it, I took the pistol out and loaded a shell into the chamber. If these creatures weren't bulletproof, they would soon be gone.

I crept down the stairs with gun in hand, ready to fire at any movement. There would be no hesitation. Whatever was in the house obviously had the ability to shape-shift. They'd already shown me my wife in two different locations, as well as mimicking one of my daughters. I didn't care if they'd changed themselves into the spitting image of the Pope, they were going down.

The downstairs was getting dark in the late evening hours. No lights had been switched on and shadows stretched out to grab anyone within their reach. The area where my wife's body had first been discovered showed no trace of it ever having been there—even the carpet was dry to the touch, not sticky with her blood. I followed the laughter to the basement door. Cracking it open, the light from below pierced my eyes like white-hot daggers, sending me a step or two backward. Gradually, my eyes adjusted, and I heard the voices of my wife and daughters talking. I listened, wanting to believe all before had been a dream. The pistol grew heavy and I dropped my arm to my side.

"Mommy, is Daddy going to be okay?"

"I'll check on him as soon as we finish this game. If he's awake, we'll all have some fun tonight. If not, I'm going to have to call an ambulance. He's going to be so mad if I do, but he's been unconscious for a long time. I'm afraid he might have really hurt himself."

So, we were going to have some fun. Yeah, right, doing what, torturing me?

Reaching above the door, my fingers skimmed along the top of the molding until they found the key I'd stored there. I closed and locked it, hoping my act would block the demons' escape plans. They'd used their evil magic to erase any trace of my wife's body, and changed my daughter into a savage beast. I couldn't take chances on bullets. There was only one answer.

I opened the hall storage closet and grabbed a bottle of lamp oil. Emptying it around the basement door, I grabbed the second bottle and splashed it on the curtains and furniture. I'd remembered reading about how burning witches at the stake was the only way to eliminate them. I prayed the same would work on demons.

Taking a cigarette from the pack in my shirt pocket, I lit it and took a long drag. Normally, my wife would nag me about smoking in the house. Now, it didn't matter. She was dead. There was no need to keep the house smoke-free, to give other demons a base to call home. There were only a couple of ounces of lantern oil left in the bottle. I poured it in the crack along the bottom of the basement door and used my shoe to scoot the liquid under it. It was my line of defense, it would keep them from approaching … from escaping.

Clicking my lighter, I set the oil aflame.

It ignited, but burned very slowly. Oil vapors began to fill the air. I grew lightheaded. There came a frantic banging at the basement door. Screams of "What are you doing?" and "Let us out, let us out!" echoed from the unseen demons behind it. I aimed the pistol and emptied it through the wood, hushing their pleading. I knew they were aware of their forthcoming death. I could feel them, hear their begging in silence for their master to come and save them. I stood guard. Today, they would die.

The flames climbed the curtains and chair covers, as wooden tables supplied the fire nourishment. I watched as it ascended the stairs, seeking more to burn. I arched back and laughed, knowing I had won. I was the survivor. The demons would be only ashes in the ruins. I would be the one enjoying life, in the future.

To do so would mean I needed to leave the house, before the flames took me away, as well.

I fought through the flames and stumbled toward the front door, oblivious to the furnace the living room had become. I recalled a warning on the lantern oil bottles about making sure it was used in a ventilated area. Its vapors had to be the reason I was so tipsy, as if I'd been drinking all day.

The hair on my arms curled and shriveled as the heat destroyed it. Cooling hands took hold of my biceps and refused to let go, then more, smaller ones, held onto my legs. I pleaded to be allowed to break free, to escape the heat that was searing my flesh, but the hands held firm. Working as a unit, they turned me around to face my captors. As my skin began to turn black, the fat spattering as bacon grease in the flames engulfing me, the spirits of my wife and children pulled me near. Her words condemned me to the fate of death—a fate they'd already discovered. "We swore to be together until death do us part. It is not right for one to live, and the other to die. Tonight, we die together."

Their hands released me, and I watched as they rose above the flames, leaving me alone to become hot ash. They had been the innocent, and I the guilty ... the insane. It was only right I stay in the flames ... for all eternity.

* * * * *

"So, did you ever see any indication that your neighbor was a violent man?"

"No, sir, we've been neighbors for a couple of years. He always seemed to be friendly. Those kids of his were brats, and his wife stuck up. She must have come from a moneyed background, or something. Why, he even waved at me while I was mowing the yard when he came home tonight. Seemed normal, not one to do such a thing. All the shots we heard, and then the smoke and fire, it just doesn't make much sense. No sir, not much sense at all."

Watching the officer walk away, Henry shook his head and walked inside his home. The fire had been a hot one—scorched the paint on his house as it burned. Now, he'd have to pay someone to come and paint his. It was a real shame.

"So, what did the police have to say?"

"Mary, you've got to stop doing this stuff. I know you like your peace and quiet, but using your Black Magic to make people see things is going too far. There are four people dead because of you. You know, I've stood by you for thirty-eight years, through good times

37

and bad. But this is going too far. Will you promise me to stop?"

"I'll do my best, Henry. But you know as well as I do, we all have our demons with which to deal. And, there's nothing like a quiet neighborhood, now, is there?"

Hungry?

My back is cooled by the damp grass as I lie staring at the stars in the night sky. The urge to kill is strong, yet I force myself to focus on the twinkling of the miniature suns, far away. Perhaps, in their surrounding orbs, a planet like this one exists—one where life has meaning, and is not taken for granted. Yes, a place where the inhabitants grace each other with harmony and good graces—not like the planet where I reside, where hate rules and life isn't worth a penny. Perhaps, the splendor the people on the other world share is as compelling as the animosity we spread amongst ourselves, on our own planet.

I chuckle. There is no such place in existence as another world, such as I envision. Hate is, and always has been, the supreme emotion, the driving force behind life itself. To love is to waddle, to become complacent. To hate is to create such intensity, one cannot help but move forward, regardless of the circumstances. It spurs our intellect to initiate action, to move us into the unknown. Dreamers love, while those who take advantage of opportunities hate. It is a fact of life, and a fact of death.

It is hate that drives me forward, not the love of peace, causing me to waste my time gazing at the heavens. I rise and shake my head at the time I've wasted. The guilt over the multiple deaths I've caused has begun to eat away at my primary purpose ... to taste another victim's warm, salty blood on my tongue, as I devour their warm flesh ... raw.

Many would be offended to hear of my pleasure. There would be no effort to understand. Yet, many of these same people would gladly devour raw fish, and pay outrageous sums to brag about the delicacies they enjoyed—later paying doctors huge amounts of money to rid them of the worms in their stomachs, caused by the same. I don't pay, nor do I have to visit doctors to eliminate the tiny white crawling bodies from inside me. Instead, I eliminate the food preparers and serve myself the freshest of meats, at times, before the victim's heart has ceased to beat.

In my early years, I remember seeing my sister in the cradle, having just arrived home from the hospital. My parents were gushing love over our new family member, ignoring the dread of sleepless nights and endless diaper changes ahead. I entertained different thoughts. Oh, she was still a sweet little baby, but in a context only I could appreciate. Her chubby little legs and cheeks, free of sinewy muscle, would melt in my mouth with each bite. My jaws relaxed and my mouth opened, in anticipation of closing upon her pale little thigh. I salivated, knowing how tender it would be to chew. I visualized myself, ripping away mouthful after mouthful, until only the gnawing away at the bone remained. Yes, I would be a satisfied young man, one who needed only to wipe away the blood from his chin and wash his fingers.

Restraining myself during those early days was exceptionally difficult. I loved fantasizing of my teeth entering flesh and tasting its delights, but hated the thoughts of my parents retaliating, should I venture too far in sating my desires. My sister was to be off limits, that was clear. But there were others from which to sample. What child hasn't been scolded in kindergarten, or early elementary grades, for a quick bite in a recess fight? My trips to the principal's office were many, as my tasting episodes were explained as "self-defense" tactics of survival against much larger opponents. I wonder to this day if several still have scars in memory of my youth?

There are not many out tonight—rare on such an inviting evening. Could this town I'm visiting have heard of the stories from my last? I would think over a hundred miles distance between would ease the fears of morbid tales of the deaths of those tempting fate in the darkness of a summer evening. Surely, a brave young person will be coming this way from a party or a date, soon. Or, am I wishing, instead of thinking straight? Could my plans have gone astray by advance warnings of my travels?

I recall my first real feast of flesh. Venturing to a party of high school buddies, uninvited, I waited in the darkness, from my perch upon a limb of a great oak tree, on the outskirts of the property. Listening to the occasional sounds below of a small animal scurrying through the brush, the peace of the dark was challenged by the party's music echoing through the trees. As happens too often, parents had trusted their sons to be upstanding citizens, and had left them without supervision for the weekend. Typical of many naïve parents versed in psychological and non-violent child-raising techniques, the boys had not disappointed their friends in displaying the failures of such practices. Popularity at stake, the two had cut no corners in supplying all the needs of their teenaged friends, to enjoy a wonderful evening of drinking and drug indulgence. As the shrieks of laughter and boisterous chatter grew more pronounced, I counted my blessings and hoped my patience would be rewarded.

Soon, a young lady exited the home, followed by a young man insistent upon her attention. Blocking her attempts to get into her car, he had chased her into the forest, in hopes of forcing himself upon her. The young lady, in her efforts to escape, easily evaded her intoxicated pursuer in the darkness. As she managed to return to her car and drive away, my breathing quickened knowing there would be no witness to tell the story later.

Hearing him stumble about in the dried leaves and underbrush, I used my highest voice to call out the name the girl had shouted several times. In a matter of seconds, his reply of "Jenny?" followed. The sharp snap of a small branch cracking, as I twisted it in my hand, drew him closer—an act I repeated several times. Standing atop the limb, I flattened myself against the tree's trunk to hide myself, becoming only another shadow in the night. Hearing him near, I removed the hunting knife from the sheath on my belt. The loud ticking of my wrist watch exaggerated itself in my mind, and I questioned if it was loud enough to alert him of my presence. My stomach churned with fear ... of failure. I had waited too long.

I began to take short, shallow breaths. He was directly under the limb upon which I stood. "I'm gonna get you, bitch ... come on, you know you want it," mumbled from his lips, ensuring his thoughts were still on the girl, instead of my discovery. As he took another step forward, I dropped, with the knife handle grasped firmly in both hands. Between gravity, my weight, and the sharpness of the blade, he stood no chance as the steel sank deep into his neck and sliced toward the spinal column. We fell forward, me scrambling atop, and pulling with all my might to remove the knife, seemingly wedged between his vertebrae. Freeing it, I sank it deep, again and again, until the sound of his breathing bubbled with blood from the blade's slits in his back—the air from the lungs seeking the easiest exit to escape.

Adrenaline pumping with anticipation, I sat straddled across his lower back. Raising the blade, I ran its flat edge across my tongue, diverting the blood upon it into my mouth. My mind exploded with ecstasy as its exquisite taste provided my taste buds with the rewards of the victor. I swallowed, the warm thickness oozing down into my stomach, providing me with a sample of what was to come. I sliced through the back of my victim's shirt from top to bottom, exposing the blood-covered flesh to the small beams of moonlight seeping through the small breaks in the leaves of the oak. I felt no need to hold back the smile crossing my face. Instead, I relished in the glory of slicing a strip of flesh from across the shoulder and stuffing it between my teeth. It was chewy, but tasty. Yet, when my victim's heart ceased its beating, a sense of sorrow overcame me. Half of the fun had been skinning and eating my prey while he had been alive. Plus, I had missed out on my greatest fantasy—cutting out the heart and eating it as it continued to pump.

I could have stayed longer and enjoyed a feast, but common sense took over. I needed to make my escape before the absence of my victim was noticed, and someone came out to search for him. I walked home, keeping myself close to the side of the road to hide in the brush from the headlights passing by. Luckily, small town traffic is minimal during the late hours, and my inconveniences were few. I came upon a stream where I swam and washed the blood from my body. Letting my blood-stained T-shirt float away with the current, it disappeared under the surface after only twenty yards or so. If later found, it would only supply information of a medium size and a familiar brand, sold to all ages. Nothing more.

My parents had been asleep when I arrived home, and my sister's records were playing their songs of teenage love and tribulations as I passed her door. I took off my stained jeans and tossed them under my bed, knowing I would bury them at the first opportunity, the next day. My neighbor's wooded lands would be the place to do so, as they only served for preserving wildlife for the nearing hunting seasons. Perhaps, in the decades to come, he would die, and they'd be sold to some developer. By then, I'd be long gone, and so would the memories of the boy murdered and skinned at a forbidden party. That is, unless they would be used as urban legends by parents in the future.

I chuckle, remembering the phrase, "There's nothing like the first time." No, there isn't. In fact, the first time one kills is filled with fear, excitement, and discovery. For most, the taking of a life isn't something often considered. Oh, there are times our anger makes us feel like killing someone for something they did to us, but seldom do we advance our actions. To experience the act of sinking a knife into living flesh with fury, over and over, and hear life exit the body, well, there's no feeling on Earth like it. I highly recommend it as a Bucket List item.

There are some things one needs to avoid, considering personal taste. I recall a young lady hiker along the Appalachian Trail who decided it better to spend the night in the company of another, instead of chancing a rare meeting with a bear alone. Not one to demand the attention of many, her lack of attractive features probably kept her safe from most human predators along the route. Oh, she was fit, but her face was a cross between a lumberjack and a garbage collector—weathered, and far from desirable. She fully enjoyed the company of conversation and laughter, and was even willing to offer herself as some sort of prize, to keep from having to sleep alone in her tent. Deciding to take her up on accompanying her inside, I quickly put my knife to use before sex became a necessity. (Even I can fantasize only so much.) The look of surprise upon her face, when the blade entered below her jaw and shot up into her brain, was a memorable one, like putting a suffering beast out of its misery. After sating my hunger on some of her flesh, and a few bites of her still-beating heart, I experimented with something I'd seen in a movie. With less effort than I imagined, I decapitated her, and then used a large rock to split her skull apart. Finishing with the coup de grace, I dug my knife in and tasted her brain. Only after the vile gray matter had touched my tongue did I remember the villain first cooking his portion, before eating. It is a mistake I will not make a second time.

The newspapers have called me a murderer, a cannibal, a ghoul, and many other names, over the years. The police consider me, according to their news releases, to be "a most heinous individual, practicing acts of revulsion to normal humans". Of course, you wouldn't expect me to agree with any of those titles or descriptions, would you? No, I am an adventurer, a connoisseur of food delights in which most ignore to indulge, a hunter of extreme tastes. Man forgets he is a predator, a survivor of the meat-eaters only by becoming one himself.

To dispose of a human life in order to supply meat affects me no more than the murdering of a cow or a pig in the slaughterhouse. They are all members of "herds" in today's world and should be treated as such. They serve no viable function, besides being food, and continuing to destroy the Earth upon which we live. Mankind is not to be loved, but hated. It is that, and the drive for food, which serves my being.

Besides, don't knock it until you try it!

Flashes

"Cease this shit!" screams my mind, in hopes my conscious state will take command and cast off the visions my dreams etch deep. Yet, even with my eyes open, the scene is clear. The mutilated bodies hang naked from the wall. Their outer skin flayed, the blood drools freely down the legs and torsos, and drips from the heads of matted hair, into puddles below each. Surprisingly, several still show signs of life.

They had struggled not long before—hoping to yank the steel hooks holding them from the wall studs. Their efforts have ceased as they concede to the agony of the extended torture. A slight moan is uttered from one. It falls only upon my ears. The ears of those lined along the wall next to her are clogged with their own drying blood. I smile, and then cringe at the sadistic urge to continue inflicting pain, begging, instead, for my sanity to flee and find solace from the evil driving my actions.

I rise, tossing aside the sweat-soaked covers of my bed. Staring at the dresser mirror across the room, I see a man haunted, his face one of despair, not rested as one should be after a night's sleep. I shower and dress. So horrible the nightmare, my need to enter the world outside of this apartment and see regular people, doing normal tasks, exceeds all other desires. Keys in hand, I leave, seeking to find the sanity I'd sent running. The sun smacks me in the face and jabs the razor-edged points of its rays into my eyes. Squinting, I locate my car and hurry to climb inside. The interior provides shade and temporarily blocks the sun's attack. I lower the visor to prevent another as I turn on the ignition. I hesitate before pulling out, pausing for a moment to catch my breath and shake the lingering shards of my nightmare from my brain.

Coffee … I need coffee. Normally, I would have made my own. Today, I cannot return inside to do so. Fear of facing the hanging bodies is unsubstantiated, but present. They exist only in my dreams, not in my real life. Yet, my confidence is in a quandary. I am an adult … a police officer. Daily, I face danger, and do so without fear. Why would a nightmare cause me to shudder and shun my own home?

My grandfather was a police officer. My father had no problems following in his footsteps, as I have no problem in following his. Environmental conditioning provides the route—we supply the manpower. It is bred within us.

Police work has changed since the days they patrolled the streets. There was always the chance of being killed, but it has increased drastically over the years. Where most criminals once drew lines as to how far they would go, the lawbreakers of our time erase them. Children have taken to being armed and using deadly force, without thinking. They are conditioned to do so by the communities and acquaintances around them, as I was conditioned to do the opposite by my family. Police officers are supposed to represent the good of the world, in the "Bad vs. Evil" scenario. Yet, public opinion fails to see it that way. Instead, we are bad guys and those breaking the law are martyrs—causes for social leaders to call out for riots and protests. They malign us in the press, throw slanderous comments and profanities without regret, and blame us when they become victims. The world has gone crazy.

Two years ago, I stopped wearing the uniform and joined the undercover unit. My job is to wander the community, find those breaking laws, and supply vital information to the uniformed officers, for them to make arrests. I am a walker of the streets, constantly on the prowl. Many of my fellow officers are not aware of who I am. Yet, I am not alone.

There are many eyes and ears residing in the land of concrete. Casual conversations, filled with information and common suffering, breeds strange friendships. I am effective in my work as I've become one of them, participating in illegal activities. I am a source for them, as I have been supplied syringes by the department. I tell the street people they are for use with insulin. They chuckle, knowing the plastic and steel tools of delivery have sent other drugs into my body, and can do the same for them. The injecting of drugs into my system is an activity I do not enjoy, but find necessary to break down the doors hiding secrets. Addicts are more prone to give out information when high. The only problem is remembering what they say when I am high, as well.

I pull my old rust bucket up to the drive-up window and take the large coffee from the hands of the pimply-faced teenager in the red and white striped uniform. The uniform exhibits the cleanliness advertised by the chain, but his dirty fingernails say otherwise. It is no matter. One cannot be picky about such things. Make a scene and you'll discover your coffee has been pissed in the next time you order.

Driving around to the other side of the fast food joint, I pull into a parking space and take a sip, nearly burning off the tip of my tongue. I've a good mind to pour it in my lap and sue the bastards. Worked before—might work again. No, I need it too bad. I can't waste it. Maybe, next time.

I stare into my rearview mirror, watching a huge, overweight lady waddle out—her arms full with coffee, a large bag of food, and a newspaper under her arm. Her destination is the car parked next to me. Our eyes meet in the mirror. I can tell she doesn't like what she sees. She hurries to get inside, thinking her car will provide safety, almost dropping her coffee as she flops down in her seat. I smile. From the size of her bag, she will probably eat three thousand calories to start her day. She sees me staring. Afraid, for some reason, she leaves quickly. I don't mind. She will have a story to tell those at work as she devours her food and wonders where she will eat lunch.

Noticing she had dropped her newspaper, I get out and snag it from the pavement. Inside the front page is a picture. It stops my breathing. The photo is of a crime scene where a family had been murdered in their own home. I close my eyes and shake my head in disbelief. The scene is a duplication of the one I had dreamed about, less than an hour before.

I wanted to vomit.

There are no bodies in the photo. Public opinion would go ballistic if they'd have shown them. But the two officers in the picture are standing in front of a wall with four hooks and blood smears. One of the officers is pointing to the floor, and the puddles of blood, as if the readers could tell it was blood in the black and white photo. I had no problem. I knew what it was.

The story below the photo speaks of how the father had been a suspected crime lord, heavy into drug distribution. Of course, the press couldn't discuss the way they'd been killed in detail, but declared the police to be stunned over the ruthless manner the killer had operated. It also stated the police had no suspects, and concluded with an editorial comment about how the police didn't push to solve such murders as it was "just another pusher" they didn't have to take to trial later.

I love how they're always so positive about the men in blue.

Seems the victims had been dead a couple of days. The children's school had asked the police to send an officer there to find out why. Yeah, another duty we've assumed over the years. Cut the school budget and the police become truancy officers. Anyway, the officer got no answer to his knocking, and became suspicious after the neighbors told him there had been no movement in the home for the last couple of days. Called it in and got permission to enter. Didn't take him long to walk back outside and puke his guts out. Poor kid, three weeks out of the academy and gets broke in this way. He'll be talking about it in the ready room for years.

Many of us have similar stories to tell. It's sad.

Tossing the paper off to the side, I called the station to check in with my lieutenant. He didn't have much time to talk. The mayor's office had seen the paper's photo and was raising hell. All concentration was on finding the murderer—and fast. I was small beans, in comparison. Told me to find out something for him, so they could get it over and done. Yeah, like I kept tabs on who was going to be murdered and by whom. So much for that conversation.

I drove the streets. Wasn't much happening. Too early in the day for action. The sun had warmed up the day and I grew a little tired. That's what not getting much quiet time will do. Damn dreams are a motherfucker to proper rest. I pulled behind a deserted strip mall and cracked the windows. Settling back in the seat, I closed my eyes for a quick nap. Was out in a matter of seconds. That's when the dream began.

I was sluggishly shuffling along the sidewalk. My mind was ordering my body to comply, but was being ignored. People around me mattered not, a fact made obvious by the way I refused to yield, bumping into several. Amid their profanities, I laughed, knowing they were only pissed because my forward progress hadn't been blocked by their imagined superiority roadblocks.

Stumbling forward, I headed toward an unknown destination. My mind went back to another time, one I didn't care to visit. I see the tears of a mother, watching as I sliced layers of flesh from her daughter with a straight razor. Cries of anguish are muffled behind the duct tape sealing her lips. She fought in desperation to free herself of her bonds, in hopes of saving her daughter. I teased, saying, "Oh, so you can't wait until I get to you? Be patient, my dear, your turn is coming soon. Right now, I just want you and your wonderful husband to experience your daughter's pain, and then your son's. I find it so much more pleasing when a family does things together, don't you?"

I refuse to speed up. I make sure they appreciate each shaving I peel from the young one's body. The muffled cries and tears flow as the blood runs in rivers, dripping silently into the dark pools it forms at my feet. Totally immersed in the task, I dare a glance at the father's eyes and lose focus. The pain and grief witnessed provides my sadistic efforts a newfound excitement. I am not stimulated by the nudity of the family, but by his mental agony. I masturbate, to further enrage him. As I climax, stars appear in the darkness and ecstasy arrives. I sat on the floor, my legs resting in the warm blood of the living and the dead, and blacked out, only to discover myself back where I had parked.

A junkie leaps at me as I leave my car. His body, weakened by lack of proper diet, is easily pushed aside and he tumbles to the piss-soaked alley pavement. He groans and rises to his knees, reaching to grasp my leg. I let him have it to the face, my knee shattering his nose. There is blood on my pant leg. Rage roars in, knowing it will stain them and I'll have to toss them away later. I am merciless, grabbing hold of his hair and beating his face to a pulp until my hand aches and knuckles split open. I come to my senses and battle an urge to retch as I see the human he once was, no longer among the living. The darkness of the nightmare overcomes me, and I fight to remain conscious.

My head clears and I'm once again stumbling along the sidewalk. I enter a familiar warehouse, with my skin crawling. I'm not an addict. I know I'm not. But the body aches for drugs as if I were. In this place, a fix has been provided many times. I know this by the multitude of used syringes cracking beneath my feet, as my weight crushes them. I wonder how many of these are mine?

My shin sends notice to my brain of its meeting with the sharp edge of a metal beam jutting out from a pile of rubbish. I fall, my palms stinging from the needles entering my flesh. I raise my hands and burst out in laughter. It is hilarious to see them dangling there. I swing them back and forth and watch as several fall free, wondering how long before the others follow. I am at my home away from home—my comfort zone.

I shake my hands, shed the remaining syringes, and rise to my feet. Just ahead and around a corner lies a door. I knock, gently at first, and then harder when there is no response. A voice from behind it hollers out for me to identify myself. It is the voice of my "friend" and supplier, Michael. I yell out my name and hear the lock click open. Recognized, he turns and walks away as I enter and follow.

"So, I've been wondering where you've been. Thought I'd lost you for a while. Did you get busted?"

I laugh at the thought. "No, I've been living the dream ... the nightmare. Need something to make it go away. You're holding, right?"

"Yeah, got some really good stuff. Will help give you good dreams, instead of bad ones. Go clean yourself up, first. There are some old clothes in the back you left the last time you were here. Looks like you got a little blood on the ones you're wearing. Have some trouble?"

I think of the junkie lying dead in the alley. "No, some fun," I reply, before going to the rear room. I shower and put on the clothes I'd left. It feels good to be clean. I am ready for a fix. I know Michael will have one waiting.

Turning to go join him, I catch sight of myself in the mirror against the wall. My face has changed from the one I woke with this morning. Now, it is one I barely recognize. It is thinner, with sunken cheeks, and there are wrinkles and dark circles surrounding the eyes. The skin, once a normal flesh tone, is now displaying a grayish hue, as if death has already arrived and is waiting on the mind to accept the fact. I spin away, disgusted at how the nightmare presents me. I know I am not like what I've seen. My eyes are playing games—tricks of sorts. I need what Michael offers.

I go to him. My steps heavy, as if the effects of the shower have worn off and the old addict phase has reappeared. I enter the room and am surprised. Michael lies back in his recliner, a needle sunk deep into his chest. His eyes are glazed—they do not blink when I pass my hand before them. I close the eyelids, knowing he is no longer going to be my "friend" ... my supplier. I will have to find another.

There is a plastic bag of good dreams on the table. It will last me until I can find another supplier. I want to partake but know I need to leave, before another arrives and I am mistaken for the one who took his life. My common sense outweighs my need. I stuff the baggie in my pocket and leave the way I entered. Pushing open the outside door, the sun has been waiting and again stabs my eyes with its rays. It is uncompromising in its wish to blind me. I close my eyes and fall back into the darkness the dream provides.

Awakening, I again find myself back in my car, behind the deserted strip mall where I'd decided to take a nap. I shudder and rub my face in my hands. I realize the nightmares are now coming to me in the daylight hours, as well as the night, as nightmares within nightmares. There is no escape from them. Although my watch shows I've been sleeping for hours, I am exhausted. Even with the windows cracked, it is stuffy and hard to breathe. I step out of the car and stretch my legs, doing my best to shake the cobwebs from my brain. I scour the area, hoping not to find a murdered junkie. There is none. Perhaps, I should make an appointment to see the department's official shrink. Just what I need, another person to tell me I'm crazy. My ex-girlfriend had already done that—a month after my ex-wife did. I'll pass. It will only get me put on administrative leave, without pay. Not what I need right now.

No, I am supposed to be finding a murderer. I drive back to the main area of action in the city and put out some feelers. Within an hour, word comes to me. No proof, but some heavy suspicions concerning a man who had been seen in the area of the family's savage attack during the prior week, and only once since—leaving the area, just before they'd been discovered.

Having a good description of the individual, I roam the streets, seeking him out. The night is different than most. Instead of those I'd become friends with being amiable, most turn away as I pass them by. Their efforts to avoid me begin to make me wonder if my cover has somehow been blown. If that's the case, I'll be back in Homicide, wearing a suit and filling out reams of paperwork, before I know it. I've grown too used to the streets. I am a part of them, not the regimented politics of the departmental offices. The transition would be hard—damn near impossible. I force myself to concentrate on finding the suspect, instead of thinking about what would be a waking nightmare.

Then, I see him. The description had been spot on—size, features, clothing—all of it matches. He is heading into a borderline residential area, one comprised of apartments and duplexes. I want to catch him with some evidence, so I stay back a block or so, watching where he leads me. Before long, he enters a duplex, off the main street and down an alley. With my ear against the front door, I hear the shrieks of children inside. There is no time to call for back up. I pull out my pistol, gather all my strength and weight, and charge at the door—ripping it from its frame.

In front of me, the man holds a young toddler, a girl of three or four years, and another clutches his thigh. Their eyes show the fear of my entrance, and of the gun in my hand. The man puts the girl down and tells them both to go to their mother. His anger is evident as he shouts for me to leave his home. He is the killer. I know it in my heart.

A figure rushes from the kitchen. It is a grown woman, carrying a butcher knife. She has evil in her black eyes. I yell for her to stop, but she refuses to yield. I shoot and watch the hole in her forehead appear—blood, brains, and skull fragments splattering the daisies on the wallpaper behind her. The man darts forward, seeking revenge. My gun coughs twice, each projectile finding its target. Their force sends his body upright and then back, bouncing off the couch before ending up on the floor. I watch as the blood oozes out from under his body and stains the carpet as it spreads.

There are voices behind me. I spin toward the door and am met with a barrage of gunfire. I feel my chest cave in as the bullets rip through my flesh. My hand goes numb and loses its grip on my pistol. I fly back and land upon an end table, by the sofa. I have no feeling in my legs, and my arms refuse to catch me as I fall to the floor, staring at the ceiling.

The voices become clearer the longer I lay there. "Yeah, we got him. But he got two more before we did. You're going to need to send a meat wagon or two. Oh, send social services, as well. There are two kids here. Yeah, they're okay, if seeing your parents killed in front of you is okay."

They have mistaken me for the killer. Yet, I still breathe. I am not dead. I need to tell them the man was the murderer, not me. I am one of them and have always been one of them—only undercover.

They continue to talk, "Lucky we got here before he killed the kids. Did you see what he did to those others? I'll never be able to get it out of my mind. I know he's a cop, but he was undercover too long. He went rogue and started killing innocent people—even skinning them. The cell phone tracking got him. If it wasn't for that, we might never have figured out who was doing it. And, that guy earlier today, a damn needle full of heroin jammed in his heart. This guy wasn't just a bad cop, he was crazy. We had to shoot him down. No telling what he would have done to us if we hadn't."

I should feel the blood flowing from my body. There should be terrible pain from my wounds. I should be writhing in agony. Yet, I am not. I know I am lying in my own bed, having a nightmare. A nightmare that will soon end. I'll awaken, get up, and start my day as I always do. Perhaps, one day, the nightmares will end.

I hope it's soon.

Trapped

My body aches. I am reminded of the pain incurred by a movie stunt man who fell onto the roof of a car to satisfy the whims of an idiotic director, or of one surviving a run through a gauntlet of boxers, each landing their best punches along the way.

I ask myself, "How can I feel so bad lying in my own bed?" Yet, I know I am not where I should be. My wife is not shutting off the ringing in my head, as she does each morning. This is not a normal day, nor am I in my normal place. I am not lying atop my mattress—not unless it has tragically turned into something harder than granite, and colder than a January wind. I didn't drink much last night. I never do. So, why is my head pounding as if I had?

I dread opening my eyes. Sooner or later I must, but I question what will happen when I do. Will I see the sun, and fall victim to having my eyes burned out of my head by its searing rays? Will I find I've gone blind, or been made that way by a sadistic ass who feels pain is what his victims deserve? Perhaps, if I open them slowly, the answer will be mine. Do I want to know the answer?

I relax my eyelids. There is no light streaming in. They begin to part—still no light. I gather my strength and open them full, ready to take in my surroundings and gauge my position. Only the darkness is with me.

Moving to leave my fetal position, I find I cannot stretch my limbs far. There are metal bars stopping them from extending further. I realize they restrain me, contain me, act as my cell, as they surround me. Kneeling, I run my fingers from their beginning, at the floor, to their meshing together at the top, as if they form a pyramid of sorts, no taller than three feet in height. I am caged as if I were a bird. My movement caused the cage to sway. It is anchored at the top, to what, I do not know. I sit, unable to stand, and try to remember what led me to this imprisonment.

Frustration takes command and I grab one of the metal rods and yank, pulling with all my strength and body weight. It doesn't move. It has been well-constructed. No amateur participated in its assembly. I repeat my act, hoping to find some flaw that might allow me hope of escape. I tell myself it cannot hold me, I am human and will find a weak spot. I test every bar of the cage's three sides. I am humbled—it proves how feeble a race we are ... how feeble I am.

Logic tells me there must be a way out of this, as I was entered into it. The cage was not constructed around my sleeping body. That thought was absurd. No, there must be a latch, a door, some way to escape. Instead of wasting my time and energy in a test of strength I have no chance of winning, I need to seek out the key to opening my cage. I begin by running my fingers along each bar, from top to bottom, seeking the slightest crack or bump indicating it might be part of an opening. My efforts are meticulous, not wanting to chance missing the one small bit of evidence that would lead to my release. Twice I rotated, hoping I'd missed something on the first. Nothing.

My brain sparked and I had an epiphany. Could I be sitting upon it? Could the metal plate, the one freezing my ass, be a door? My fingers slide against the plate, again seeking any sign of an existing crack. Once, twice, three times I run them across the top, with no results. I use my fingernails to do the same, praying they'll catch the edge of some small gap I had missed. Finding none, I stretched them through the bars and did the same to the underside of the plate, at least as far as they would reach. Still no latch or hint of an opening. My resolve dwindling, I sat to contemplate my next move.

"Having a hard time finding your way out, are you?" The words blasted me from all sides.

"You can turn down the volume. I'm not hard of hearing," I yell back. It is a voice I've heard before, but can't remember where. It reminds me of a time, perhaps an experience, I've tried to forget, to erase from my memory.

"Do you know why you're here?" The words seek my response … they demand it. "Do you have any recollection of the events that took place, prior to your arrival?"

My mind races, doing its best to recall. My memory is on vacation. I remember nothing more recent than being at the office, yesterday afternoon. The day had been a nightmare, starting before I had tasted my first cup of coffee. Last minute demands had everyone rushing about as if the world was about to end and we had to prepare. I smiled, remembering my boss' face, so fearful of failing and losing her high paid job, frantic in pushing the rest of us to work faster. And, that was it, nothing else crossed the void into the present.

"You seem to be stalling," the voice accused, none to amiably. I cover my ears to protect them from the piercing volume. My head throbs and threatens to explode. "Think of what you remember last, and move forward. It's simple."

I focus my efforts on his words and their meaning. They do not help. Instead of remembering, I focus on my current situation. I am being held hostage, a prisoner in a cage—but for what purpose? Not only is my captor using the metal bars to hold me, but also the darkness. I am the victim of his sadism, his game playing. It is not to my liking.

I shiver, goosebumps rising on my bare skin. My legs are protected by some type of elastic-waisted pants, and a short-sleeved pullover covers much of my torso, neither supplying much protection from a dropping room temperature. The metal plate is attempting to freeze my bare feet. It is winning the battle—they are so numb I can barely feel my toes. I recall the Yoga Lotus position my wife used to meditate and try to duplicate it, in order to protect them, but find I am not as flexible as she. Through the material of my pants, the cold is seeping as well. I lie on one side, in order for the other to warm as much as possible, before switching over to do the same for the other. The signs of hypothermia are present as I find comfort in the darkness of my mind. I no longer feel the cold. I am escaping into a world of dreams.

"Wake up!"

I am groggy, yet conscious. Almost saddened to find myself still prisoner, I again shield my ears from the booming of the loudspeaker. Why the torture? Just turn the damn thing down!

"You need to remember. Stop avoiding it. Where was the last place you remember? We will not tolerate your silence any longer."

"Why are you torturing me?" I scream, my anger rising. "I've done nothing to deserve this!"

"But you have … you have. It is essential you remember."

Remember? Who could remember, dealing with the temperature changes you people are putting me through? The freezing had been replaced by excessive heat, and my left side is sizzling against the metal plate. I sniff to see if I am reaching "Medium" or "Well Done" status. Strange, there is no aroma.

I'm ignoring the banter coming from the speakers. It is useless to me, ignorant dribble doing nothing to relieve the incessant heat. Sweat drips from every pore and bubbles upon the metal beneath me. My insides are roasting and will soon be done enough, the cannibals using the speaker will soon be able to serve them as a dinner entrée. My lungs are scorched from breathing the air around me. I am lightheaded, reaching out for the darkness I found in the cold, in hopes of it saving me from the blistering of the metal plate. Falling forward, my forehead touches the bars and a shockwave blasts me into the darkness I'd sought. Yet, the quiet I'd found before escapes me. The voice followed me and gives me no peace.

"You must face the truth. There is no escape allowed."

I wake, still in darkness, but there is no longer a metal plate below. Instead, I feel the cool chill of concrete. I have been released. I am stretched out flat, my body relishing the freedom of movement. I rejoice. Opening my mouth to announce it to the world, the pain of parched lips cracking ceases the celebration. My body craves water, any type of liquid, to nourish the dried shell of a human I have become.

"I repeat, you must face the facts. There is no other option!"

I try to rise. My body is still stiff from being caged so long. From a kneeling position, I force myself higher. I am standing, but for how long is questionable. A wave of dizziness strikes, and I feel as though I may quickly return to the darkness which has become my friend. It passes and, though wobbly, I manage to stay upright. I extend my arms and inch my way forward until my fingers brush against a wall. It is firm, ungiving to any pressure I use, yet feels as if it is a plastic material.

Keeping one hand against it, and the other in front of me, I slide along until I feel the next. I turn and do the same once again ... and again ... until I have completed the square. I then reach as high as I can, my fingers unable to find the top. I am still in a cage. This time, it is larger, at least ten feet square. As before, no hint of an exit exists.

"Unless you remember, you will stay here forever."

I cannot escape the voice. It echoes in the darkness and reverberates within my skull. Covering my ears is useless. Uninvited, it still finds a way inside. I am helpless against it.

A drop of water falls to my face. Now, I question my sanity. There are no stars or moon above. How can I feel a raindrop? It is followed by another, and then more. I open my mouth in quest of sating my driving thirst. My lips welcome the moisture and soon flex without cracking wider, as the drops become a steady downfall. Within seconds, my shirt and pants are soaked, and my hair hangs in my face. I shed my clothes and allow my body to soak in the blessed water, washing off the sweat from my previous temperature encounter. I fill up my mouth and swallow until my stomach has swollen and can hold no more.

The speakers blare something about how I will suffer if I continue to ignore their commands. I care not. My head is clearing, and my body is refreshed. I know the water isn't rain, but runs from pipes to feed into my new cage. What once was pleasurable is now painful, as the force of the water landing upon me has increased. Each drop has become a stinging pellet, peppering my bare body. I kneel and splash about, seeking the clothes I'd shed. Though not thick, they would present some buffer to ease the impacts. The water has not drained, only accumulated, and is now almost knee-deep. I am lucky to find my shirt and don it quickly, the pants following within seconds. The pressure increases once more, and the pellets now hit hard, as marbles from a slingshot would. I duck below the surface of the water, in hopes it will protect me. I stay as long as I can, rising above only to catch a quick breath before going back under. The water, once cool, is decreasing. My mind drifts to a movie about an ocean liner sinking after having hit an iceberg. I wonder if my lips are turning as blue as those who died that night.

The downpour ends. I am up to my neck in freezing water. Soon, I will succumb to hypothermia, as I have already done once here. If lucky, I will not awaken. I am tired of the torture. I am ready to die.

"I must warn you for the last time, tell me where you were last. Admit it, and come to grips with it ... you will be saved. Otherwise, I make no promises."

The words are clear, but my response does not come. I don't remember where I was, or what I was doing, before my arrival here ... wherever I am. I know I should be home with my family, eating our dinner, and enjoying an evening together. Or, could it be I should be sitting at my desk at the office? I don't know what time it is, or what day, I only realize I've been here too long. I've survived all they've put me through and should feel proud. Yet, there is no pride, only weariness. I want it over and done. I want the end.

The water level is going down. Somewhere, the water is draining out. If I could only find where it flowed out, perhaps I could find an exit close by. I dive below the surface again and strive to find which direction the current flows. I can locate none. It is as if the floor has turned into a giant sponge and is absorbing all the water. Only puddles remain. I continue to shiver, sitting in my wet clothes. I huddle into a ball, attempting to find warmth within the closeness of my body parts. If only the warmth of the sun on a summer day were present. No one shivers sitting next to a pool in July.

A hum of electric motors begins above me. The darkness hides what is happening, but I fear not. It is useless to prepare, useless to brace myself, when I know not for what to brace. The voice demands I speak. I demand it leave me alone. Neither of us pays attention to the other.

I flinch as something brushes against my face. I reach out and grab hold. The feel of a cold bare wire is there. Another touches my leg and another my arm. It is as if I have entered a spiderweb of wires. I struggle to free myself of their touch, but they return, their numbers increasing tenfold.

A loud popping noise fills my ears and I am sent flying to the floor. Before I can rise, another follows and my body arches high, out of control. I hear the sound a final time and I begin to fade away, hopefully for the last time.

I am caught between worlds, the living on one side, and the dead on the other. Evil laughter and claws pull me into their realm, as I fight to maintain my hold against their efforts. There are other voices, voices of humans talking above me. I hear their words as I slip away, the laughter swallowing me.

"So, do you think the shock therapy worked?"

"Only time will tell. He's been living inside himself so long, it's the last resort."

"It's so sad that he can't free himself from his own guilt. What a tragedy. Can you imagine being drunk, having an accident, and watching your family die around you? He'll have to live with that forever. Plus, he was trapped in the only part of the car that wasn't submerged in the icy river. Took hours for the crews to get him free. No wonder he's in such a state."

"Well, if it doesn't help him today, we can do it again next week. He's not going anywhere. We'll keep him as long as it takes to make him better. Besides, he's better off here, than caged up in some prison. Don't you agree?"

Now, I Wait

Most Baby Boomers are fans of clowns. Memories of Emmett Kelly and Bozo filling our childhood with laughter are held dear to our hearts, as are the nameless circus clown troops rollicking about, while spraying seltzer water at each other and tossing buckets filled with confetti into the audience. Many of us still wonder how so many fit into the tiny car they would drive into the center ring, and the endless number exiting it.

Thirty or forty years ago, everything changed. Suddenly, people started dreading clowns and expressing their fears over the men in funny make-up. No longer were they viewed as supreme court jesters, but as demons, and evil in hiding. Perhaps Hollywood's efforts to find new villains played a big part. Maybe it was the news, showing John Wayne Gacy dressed in his clown outfit to entertain children, and then finding out he'd murdered thirty-three young men. Or, could it have been during that period in history, people changed. Instead of looking for the good in people, they began looking for the evil in everything around them? It appeared America had lost its sense of humor, and allowed hate to grab hold.

I've collected clown memorabilia as a hobby for decades. I have a special room devoted to clown lamps, posters, statuettes, costumes, and many other items associated with the bringers of laughter throughout the years. When I feel depressed or, if I just want to make myself smile, you'll find me in this room being cheered up by my "toys".

As a collector, I attend auctions to find the best buys. People on the internet tend to think their items are worth ten times more than they are. Auctions are always more reasonable. In fact, a few weeks ago, I was able to purchase an antique make-up kit that had belonged to a Western European circus clown. I remember chuckling when the auctioneer gave up trying to pronounce the owner's name and sputtered out, "Some damn German's kit" as a description. For my bid of twenty dollars, I walked out with what I believed was a real treasure.

Getting it home, I emptied the contents upon my desk for closer inspection. Obviously, someone had already done so, and taken the best of the bunch. The few containers and tubes remaining held only dry or hardened contents. Still, it proved they were indeed parts of the original kit, and not duplicates later added. Working to clean a metal tag by the handle, I found it engraved with the owner's name, Heinrich Batenhorst. My curiosity grew.

Over the next few days, I researched the name on the web, and at the university library. In an old book with yellowed pages, information was finally found. Heinrich had been a famous clown in the German circus, back in the pre-World War II days. His fame came from being a somewhat sadistic magician, before using his humor to please the audience. This aided in him becoming a favorite entertainer of the Nazi Party's social events. He had even received high praise from Adolf Hitler for his act, and the mysticisms it included.

As Germany began its invasion of Europe, Batenhorst supported Hitler, and continued to entertain the troops. Yet, in 1943, things began to sour for Hitler, and his paranoia initiated extreme investigations. The German elite, loyal party supporters, and, of course, borderline party members were questioned, and many were sent to concentration camps. Heinrich managed to flee from Germany, but was caught attempting to board a plane in France, with a flight plan to London. The SS immediately listed him as a traitor and sentenced him to be shot. Still, he entertained the guards with his act until the day they came to execute his sentence. All his cell contained was his make-up kit. He had vanished.

No one had seen him since.

Back home, I sat staring at the case upon my desk. I was looking at a piece of history. Somehow, this kit had survived the Nazi scourge, and all since. I shook my head in annoyance. If only I could find out more about what it had endured since the day of Heinrich's disappearance. Who had carried out the case, where had it traveled, how many had owned it since, and what secrets could it tell, if it could speak? The twenty dollars had been a small sum for such an item. I had, indeed, been lucky in finding it.

Yet, the more I studied the kit, the more something seemed wrong. I studied the exterior, and then opened it and inspected the interior. I hadn't noticed prior, but the dimensions didn't coordinate. The inside was smaller—not as deep as one would expect. Contents emptied, I tipped over the case and tapped the bottom, while my other hand felt for the vibrations inside. The wooden slats along the bottom were solid, but not so much as to reduce the vibrations of the tapping. I searched the bottom for some sort of release button, even trying to move the slats one direction or another, for entry. Nothing. Doing the same to the sides, a slat gave way and slid up, less than an inch, giving me access to a finger-hold of another slat on the bottom. Lifting it, the slat fell off to the side. There lie a few pieces of aged paper, folded as a letter, and a small black cloth bag.

Careful not to cause the brittle paper to crack, I unfolded the paper. Although the writing was elegantly done, the words were unfamiliar to me, as they were written in German. This would be only a temporary setback, as I could easily have one of my friends at the university translate them in a day or two. Setting it aside, I turned my attention to the small bag. Untying the string at the top, I tilted the bag down and out dropped a huge golden ring, with a black opal stone. Bouncing it in my palm, I discovered it to be extremely heavy for its size. Too small to fit my primary ring fingers, I wondered how small a person would have to be, to have it fit properly. Still curious, I took a chance and tried it on my pinky finger. It fit!

I admired its beauty as it reflected the glow of the desk lamp's bulb, but immediately began to feel lightheaded. It was if I was in a whirlpool, without benefit of a life preserver. Lights flashed in the surrounding darkness and I landed in a chair, with a club table sitting in front of me. My mouth dropped open as I found myself in a cabaret of decades ago. There were no electric lights, only antique oil lamps, filling the room around me with heavy fumes and excess heat. The crowd around me was laughing and speaking loudly over the band's music, many wearing military uniforms with swastikas. Upon the stage, scantily clad ladies danced around a clown waving his arms as if to send them away. No, this wasn't a happy-faced clown of my childhood memories, but instead, one with a frowning face that exhibited an aura of intrigue and mystery. Choreographed kicks and misses at the dancers leaving the stage drew many more laughs, but the clown didn't smile. No, he was pacing back and forth, leaning over, as if looking at the floor with his arms behind his back. Alone on stage, he turned to the audience, stood at attention, and shot out his arm in a military salute shouting, "Heil Hitler!" Many stood to return the salute, shouting the same.

Not sure how to proceed, the audience silenced itself, awaiting his direction. Searching the audience, one could feel the tension start to build. Only when his eyes met mine did the band begin to play once more, breaking the suspense of the moment. Exiting the stage, he worked himself through the crowd, bouncing to the rhythm of the band, until he was a few feet from me. Leaning over until his face was only a few inches away from my own, his hot breath burned my face, and his eyes began to ooze blood down his cheeks. I was paralyzed, not with fear, but as if he had transformed me into a statue. Yet, with each drop of Hell's blood that dripped upon his chest, my own felt their burning heat sear my flesh.

I wanted to wipe away the pain, but was still unable to move. He roared with laughter and spun around to demonstrate his handiwork to the cheering crowd. I wondered what they could find so amusing, as he'd done nothing to me they could witness. The glow of dancing flames broke through the shadows in front of me and reflected in the glass before me. I was on fire! Still, I was helpless to fight the illusion. My muscles were locked tight. Braving the flames, he leaned forward and his lips whispered into my ear, "Thank you. I've been waiting so very long for you to arrive."

His lips kissed my forehead, scrambling my brain and providing visions of mass killings and executions in concentration camp ovens. Prisoners were being skinned alive, and their outer layers being used to make lampshades. German officers with "SS" on their collars were laughing as they rotated around me—fingers pointed, as if I were to be their next victim. I fought to move, to escape, and screamed with all my might!

I woke at my desk, sweat dripping from my chin onto the black bag. I ripped off the ring and flung it to the desktop, not caring if it was damaged in the process. Scooting back, I sought a safe zone, a distance where it could no long affect me, or my mind. I was exhausted, frustrated, and filled with unanswered questions. What type of spell did this hunk of gold and black stone cast upon me? Was I chosen, or simply the one who had loosed it upon myself by slipping it on my finger? Was my vision a dream, or had it really occurred?

I left the room and closed the door behind me. I wanted nothing more to do with the ring—only to sleep. The vision had drained all the energy from my body. Even shuffling to the bedroom was a chore. Yet, sleep avoided me. I tossed and turned all night, finally giving up on seeking the solace of slumber upon the sun's arrival. I showered, dressed, and fed my dog before heading to work.

Not far from the house, the yellowed pages of the letter lying on my desk came to mind. Giving in to my curiosity—more of an obsession—I returned home. Reaching for the pages, a glint of the sun's rays shining upon the ring caught my attention. The urge to put it on was tremendous. I reached for it, but pulled back, fearing a repeat of the night before. I placed the letters in a file folder and hurried from the room. Only when I was back in the car did I find myself far away enough to escape the ring's magnetism.

I arrived at the university's language department and sought out my old friends. As luck would have it, none were around. Desperate, I located a student who volunteered to translate the letter for a twenty-dollar bill.

What a waste. The letter was a sham—nothing more than a story of Faust, told in the style of the 1930s.

Disappointed, going to work was the last thing I wanted to do. My thoughts of finding out the mystery of the ring were at a standstill, without the letter providing me any hints. I needed answers, but had no way of finding them. Maybe the ring held them. Perhaps it was engraved on the inside or something. The hell with going to work—I had to find out.

Walking in the house, I was surprised at my dog's absence. Chester normally met me with tremendous enthusiasm, begging me to take him for a walk in the sunshine. I hollered out his name, hoping the Irish Setter would come bounding around the corner. Instead, a light whimper sounded from the kitchen. Rushing to his side, I knelt beside where he was lying. He was so weak he could barely raise his head enough for my hand to slide underneath.

"You, poor boy … what could have brought this on? Have you been into something you shouldn't have?"

I searched around the kitchen for any sign of anything he could have eaten that could have led to his present condition. None of the cabinets containing cleaning items were open, and I had no plants he could have munched on. We had enjoyed a day at the park over the weekend. Could he have picked up some sort of ailment from another animal there? Regardless of the cause, I had to get him help.

I ran to my desk to find the name of the vet I'd taken him to for his shots a couple of months before. They'd been kind and quick, and Chester seemed to enjoy the workers there. I dug into my drawer, seeking the receipt that would have their address and office phone number. Ah, there it was—now I could get him assistance. I set the receipt down and pulled the phone close.

That's when my finger brushed against the ring.

The mere touch of the cold metal on my skin rekindled my obsession. I fondled it between my index finger and thumb, enjoying the warming sensation it sent through my body. Ignoring everything else, I stared at its beauty and allowed it to cast its spell. I loved this ring, more than life itself. But, shaking the sanity back into my head, I remembered the one thing I loved more—Chester!

Tossing the ring to the other side of the room, I picked up the receipt to find the phone number of the vet he needed. I picked up the phone and dialed frantically. Just as they answered, Chester appeared in the doorway—wagging his tail.

Speechless, I hung up.

Trotting over to the ring, he pawed at it, as if to put it on. He was acting normally, as if he'd never been ill. He lay on his stomach and used his nose to push it around, like his favorite soup bone. My elation at his immediate recovery was replaced with my concern the ring had affected him, as it had me.

That's when there was a bark from the doorway. There stood Chester, wagging his tail!

I shot my glances back and forth between the two canines. Mass confusion filled me—two Chesters didn't make any sense. Which one was Chester, and which one was the imposter? And, most importantly, what the hell was the imposter, anyway?

Catching the ring on one of his claws, Chester's body began to vibrate, to blur and transform. A rumbling filled the room, and the house began to shake, as the form grew larger. Gradually, the four-legged creature in front of me became a man—a man I recognized.

"I do hope you'll excuse me," the figure before me whispered in a heavy German accent. "I needed time to adjust to this time and place. I've spent so very long away from this world."

The magician from my vision, the owner of the ring, Heinrich Batenhorst, stood before me. I had so many questions to ask, but found myself once again paralyzed. My body didn't have the strength to fight, as it had the night before. I was being drained of energy.

"In a few minutes, I'll be strong enough to begin to live once more. I spent so many years in that box, hiding from the Nazi murderers. It cost me my soul, but I'm hoping it was worth it. There's so much to learn about this future world. Your home is filled with so many new contraptions. It may take me a while to learn how to operate them, but I'll enjoy every second of it."

The real Chester walked over to me and stared up ... confused. He sniffed at me and let out a sad whimper, as if saying his last goodbye to me. He rose, his front paws on my knees, and nuzzled my chin. In his eyes, I saw my reflection. It was blurry, as if it were reforming itself into that of another. My features were fading. I was becoming almost transparent!

"Yes, I see you've discovered your body is now becoming my body. It's a standard function of the ring. I'd give you my old one, but I had to use it for the ring to work the first time. Damn thing turned to ash as I took refuge from the Nazis, in the ring. Now, your spirit will take residency there. One day, you may find one that will assist you in escaping, as I have. Of course, it may require you selling your soul to the devil, but I'm sure you'll agree, it will be worth it."

There is only darkness. No days—only an endless night, without rest. Time has no meaning as eternity may be my fate. Now, I can only wait—wait for some poor soul to be as foolish as I was.

I have not been approached for the selling of my soul. Perhaps, Hell doesn't want me. Besides, Hell could provide no torture greater to that I am enduring. I'm sure the magician has started a new life. With his powers, he will not need to assume my old one. I'm sure he probably made his contract filled with clauses to keep him young until he grows bored with living.

Two days ago, I loved the laughter clowns brought. Their antics and smiles fooled me and fed my naïve outlook about those who hide their evil under the make-up they wear. Those who disguise true intentions with laughter.

The laughter of madness.

The Drive

We've all had them—Hell Weeks—those where no amount of money is worth the trials and tribulations you endure. The times frustrations get too great and you go online seeking a new career, knowing you'll not find anything worth pursuing. All they provide is a chance to find another employer wanting to find an idiot who will believe their lies long enough to be taken advantage of. Then be fired for some reason they cannot validate, but embellish enough you won't win in court if you file charges against them.

Unless you want a ten dollar an hour telemarketing position.

No one ever said the construction industry would be easy. There are always setbacks, and problems hitting you when least expected. The rain had been the major culprit this last week, making a mud pit out of our work area. It wasn't a normal mud, something you'd watch two beauties wrestle in while drunk, it was the sticky type, adhering to everything it touched. Moving around the site was a nightmare, regardless if you were in a front loader, or on foot. In addition, the state inspectors had shown up, without prior notice, doing their duty to delay our schedule by investigating every bolt before the next one could be locked in place. Eight-hour days had turned into twelve-hour ones, just to maintain some semblance to their planning. The two-day weekend of rest would be greatly appreciated.

Driving home, I did my best to forget about work and look forward to a peaceful evening with the wife. Dinner, a movie, and then sleep ... endless sleep, until the morning came and the wife demanded I rise and do some ridiculous chore she had on her damn "To Do" list. Oh, to be single again!

I undressed on the back porch, as I always do after work, especially when my clothes are covered with mud. My plans were to rinse them off with the hose the next day, and then stick them in the washer. Maybe after two or three wash cycles, they'd begin to resemble something close to being clean. My boots would have to be hosed off, as well. They stank like three-day old roadkill, lying in the heat of an Alabama summer. Once showered, I slipped on some sweats and joined the wife for dinner. So far, the evening was going as I'd planned.

We finished eating and stuck a movie in the disc player. Just as it was about to get through the opening credits, my phone rang. I seldom answer after ten o'clock, as late-night phone calls have a habit of being wrong numbers or bad news. Seeing a friend's number, I took a chance.

Guess what? Yeah, bad news, of sorts. No words, just moaning and groaning. Not like during sex, but more like a person in terrible pain. I kept asking what was going on and if he was okay. Finally, he answered me with, "Please, come help me," right before the phone went dead. I called him back several times, but got only his voicemail.

I set the phone down, wondering what to do. He had recently moved over two-hundred miles away for a new job, so helping him was going to take some doing. I called the police department in his town, but they told me the address I'd given them wasn't any good. Seemed the place had burned down some years back. Hanging up, I shook my head and tried to concentrate on the movie the wife was enjoying. Unfortunately, his words ringing in my head didn't let me do the same.

Before the movie ended, I was in the bedroom packing an overnight bag. I wasn't going to drag my wife along, but I had to go see what was wrong. Somehow, I had to find him and make sure he was okay.

"So, do you really think you're going without me?"

Within fifteen minutes, the wife had packed a couple of bags and we headed down the road. She had refused to let me go alone, saying we spent too much time apart, as it was. I didn't mind her tagging along, and kept my fingers crossed I wasn't getting her into a mess of some sort.

The radio did a good job of keeping us awake for a while, but Sheila dozed off about halfway there. The interstate was so monotonous, exit signs and white lines, nothing else. I tried calling my friend a couple of times, but had the same results as earlier. I'd misjudged how exhausted I was, and convenience store coffee was of little assistance in my battle to keep from dozing off.

That is when my phone started ringing.

I answered, but got only static. The number had been that of my friend. I began to wonder how bad he could be injured if he was unable to speak. Expressing my concern to my wife, who had been awakened by the phone's ringing, I was slightly put off by a tear running down her cheek.

"I know you liked Jason, but I didn't know you liked him enough to cry for him."

"He's a good friend," she whispered, almost apprehensive in continuing. "I knew him long before you and I got together."

"How well did you know him," I responded, knowing what I was going to hear wasn't going to be liked. "Was it enough to go to bed with him?"

Her silence told me the answer.

We continued our drive without talking, both of us consumed by our thoughts. I've always been the jealous type, and didn't like the idea of just finding out she'd had a relationship with Jason. We'd gone places and enjoyed concerts and sporting events as a trio, many times. I thought it because he and I were friends. Obviously, there was much more to it.

My phone alerted me to a text message—*Ten more miles. Tell Sheila I'm sorry.*

"So, what does Jason have to be sorry about?"

She turned away and watched out her side window. "I'm not sure," she whispered, trying to keep her voice from cracking. "I just hope he's okay."

"Just out of curiosity, when was the last time you and Jason made love?"

She began to cry, sniffling at first, but it turned into an outpouring of emotion in a matter of seconds.

My phone received another text—*Six more miles.*

I wanted to control my anger, to act as if I didn't understand, to be the forgiving husband who believed anyone could make a mistake, and forgive them for doing so. Instead, my stomach churned, and I came close to throwing up. The woman I'd married only a few months ago, was cheating on me.

What a piece of trash. So much for wedding vows.

Another text—*Get ready to stop real soon.*

How did he know where we were at? Was he tracking us, somehow? The interstate was empty at this late hour—no cars or trucks in sight, in either direction. I turned on my bright lights and saw skid marks leading off the road. Pulling over, Sheila jumped from the car and ran down the embankment. I followed, enraged to hear her calling out his name. She slipped on the damp grass and fell back, her head slamming against the ground. She lay stunned and barely conscious, when I reached her.

"Jason, is that you Jason?"

I had no doubt, it was Jason she wanted to save her, not me. I lifted her in my arms and continued to the pick-up truck, now visible in the moonlight, fifty yards away. Opening the passenger side door, I set her in the seat and walked around to check out the motionless body behind the wheel. Yeah, it was Jason—dead as could be—his face smashed and caved in beyond recognition. He must not have been wearing his seatbelt, as the front glass was cracked directly in front of him.

Standing there, my thoughts ran through all I'd found out. I had to decide if I still wanted to be with a woman I couldn't trust, or go through a divorce. My construction company was just getting off the ground, and I hated to lose part of it in a divorce settlement, yet I'd given my word to take care of her.

Walking back around to the passenger's side, I reached inside, took hold of the back of her head, and slammed her forehead against the windshield with all my strength. Then, I wrenched her head around until I heard the spine pop. Her breathing stopped and she went limp. As a final act, I thrust her face into his crotch, right where it belonged.

I know, to forgive is Godly. Well, I never was much of one for religion. I am one for being honest and true to the one you commit to—unlike Sheila. I returned to my car, grabbed her bags, and put them in the truck cab. If anyone asked, which I'm sure they would do, I'd just tell them she decided to leave me and go away with Jason. The convenience store where I'd purchased coffee was only one of many, forty miles back. I doubted the police would go back and check videos from all the ones in between.

I drove ahead to the next exit and made a quick return, heading back home. As I reached the spot across the road from where their bodies sat, my phone received another text. I gave it a quick glance and had to pull off the road. Sitting there, I stared at the words--*Thank you for bringing us together.*

Yeah, it had been a week from Hell. Probably just a sample of what I've got to look forward to one day. Little old matchmaker me ...

Fuck it!

Shhh! Hush!

Shhh! Please, don't say a word, cough, or move a muscle. Just stay down under that bush, and don't dare get up.

Hear the crackling of the leaves over there? Yeah, they're coming. I don't know what they are—never seen anything like them in any schoolbook. Kind of reminds me of a cross between a bear and a wolf, but they growl more like a mountain lion. Big suckers ... when they raise up on their hind legs, they're over eight feet tall. They can run on two legs, but most of the time I've seen them running on four. They run faster that way. Watched one of them outrun a deer, one afternoon. Overtook it in fifty yards, jumped on its back, and snapped its neck with its jaws.

Yeah, they've got long-ass teeth, not like a sabre-toothed tiger, more like a wolf on steroids. Sons of bitches go crazy when they eat, ripping and tearing away until they get through the hide, and then almost inhaling huge strips of meat. Not like most creatures, at all. They don't want an audience while they're devouring their food. Nope, watched one eye a hungry fox who was just sitting there waiting on scraps. Sucker didn't like it at all. Took out after that fox and twisted the head right off him. Then, went back to eating, like nothing had happened.

What are you doing here, anyway? Didn't you see the No Trespassing signs? This here is private property—

belongs to me. I'd beat the tar out of you, but then they'd know where we are hiding. Oh, they got a good idea, I'm sure. I've seen their noses in the air plenty of times, sniffing about, trying to catch my scent. If you're going the same direction as the wind, and they're behind you, they can't tell where you're at. Had one chase me all the way to the cabin a while back. I was scared to death. The door shook every time it pounced against it. Thought it was going to give way, but it held. If it hadn't, I wouldn't be here now, would I? I stayed inside for a couple of days. I knew it was out there, waiting on me to show myself. At night, I could hear the growls rumbling outside. It probably could have busted through the windows, but they're so small, I don't think it could have fit through them.

Shhh! Seriously, you got to be quiet when the leaves stop rustling. That means he's stopped and is listening, trying to figure out which way to go next. Hush, now, just stay still, and don't say a word. Maybe he'll go off, away from us. I hope so. Be still. I'll tell you when it's okay to move.

Okay, I think I hear him heading off. Could be just a ploy, though, so be patient. If he doesn't see or hear anything in a minute, going that way, he may come back. Sometimes, the best offense is no offense. Last summer, I sat under a fallen tree for a full day, and most of the night. Had a damn copperhead crawl right over my legs. I didn't bother it, and it didn't bother me, just kept crawling the direction it wanted to go. I'd rather take a bite from one of them, than to chance meeting up with one of those big guys.

Listen! Hear that? He's coming back this way. I told you they do that sometimes. They figure if their prey thinks they've given up, the prey will believe it's safe and head off. It's like a game to them, and they're damn good at it. Ain't gonna beat them, I tell you, not if you give them any hints to where you might be at all. They're pretty damn smart.

Shhh! I can hear him getting closer. He's back by that big oak tree down the path. If he comes by us, you better freeze every muscle in your body, and hold your breath for as long as you can. Last thing we want is for him to get hold of us. Why, I've heard tales where they rip off a person's arms and legs and let them watch while they eat the meat, before finally killing the poor bastards. Can you imagine, sitting there watching your limbs being eaten? What could you do ... wiggle ... tell them you were going to call the police ... sue them?

Bet you'll pay attention to the No Trespassing signs, next time, won't you?

You seem kind of nervous. Well, you got a right to be. First off, you get caught by me for being here when you aren't supposed to be, and then we come across one of these bastards. I'm tough to deal with, but there's no dealing with them. I've heard tales where they bit the head of a stranger right off, and spit it up against a rock. It's still there, as far as I know. No one wants to take the chance of getting it. Why, if one was to bite off your head, I wouldn't give two hoots in Hell about trying to get it. Why would I? Damn thing wouldn't do me a bit of good. If someone found me with it, they'd try to blame me for killing you. Then I'd be in jail, where you should be for trespassing on my land.

Oh, there would be some folks who would believe me. I ain't the only one to see these things. Fact is, they're kind of common in certain areas, around here. Most of us living around here know where to stay out of, to keep from running into one of them. In my forty-odd years in the area, I've figured them out a little. We show them respect, and they don't bother us ... much. Occasionally, one will be mad over something and come after us, but most of the time we can go about our business, like normal folk. Not folks like you, who don't pay attention to signs, but good folk who do what's right.

Wouldn't know about that, though, would you? You're probably one of those rich city fellows, who think they can do as they want because they got a little more money than most. Why don't you go out and offer some of that cash to one of these creatures? Then, you'll find out exactly how much good it will do you. Your head might get a chance to watch him wipe his butt with it, after he stuffed himself with your arms and legs.

Well, I think he's gone now. Notice that stink in the air is gone? Yeah, those suckers smell worse than my outhouse does. The way the wind's blowing, we'd smell him if he was still close. Want to stand up and see if he's still around? No? Why? Are you a chicken shit coward? What if I told you there was a copperhead right by your ass, coiled and ready to strike? Yeah, I thought that would get your tail up! No, ain't no copperhead there. Look around while you're up. You see anything? Nothing? Well, just stand there a minute or so. Oh, you might want to lay your rifle down. The sight of one makes them crazy. Just thought I'd let you know. Hate for you to cause one to charge us. Wouldn't stand much of a chance, now, would we? Besides, you can always buy another rifle, if you get out of here alive, can't you?

Go on now, be as quiet as possible and get back to your car or truck, or whatever the hell you drove up here in, and get out of here. Hurry, you don't want to be around when it comes back. Don't run, just walk a steady pace. You ought to be all right. Maybe, you'll have a story to tell. Don't bring any of your friends back up here, though. I won't be as nice to you, if you do. May even try to lead one of these creatures to your group. Be fun to watch him take out the lot of you. Now, go! Scat!

Damn, watch the asshole run. Should be hearing a scream in a minute or two. Oops, there it is already. Son of a bitch was closer than I thought. I hate hearing those screams, though. Wish he'd just rip off the head and shut him up. Thank you! I was worried you'd do the arms and leg thing again, and he never would shut up. Now that you're busy eating, I can get back to my cabin. God, I hate damn city folk who think they're better than everyone else. Glad to see the bastard find out the rest of us ain't as dumb as they think. Hang on, old man, I don't want to forget this nice rifle. Looks like it's brand new. I'll hold on to it a while, and then sell it next spring. Should bring me a good price.

One of these days, I'm gonna have to put up a new No Trespassing sign. The old one fell down a year or so ago. Been meaning to do that, but these creatures tend to leave me alone, as long as I keep feeding them. Kind of a mutual respect thing. I'm glad to do it for them. Anything for a friend, or for a creature who can eat you.

Right?

Together

I miss your laughter.

My heart is breaking, but I will survive. I always do. It's not that I want to keep going on without you, but I have no other choice, besides considering suicide. Even though our time together was short, I'm sure that would not be your wish for me. Your understanding and love of life would cast those thoughts aside, in an instant, just as I now must do.

I recall the day we met. I was so frightened to come closer, afraid I might say or do something that would send you away, laughing at my nervousness and feeble attempt to build up the courage to begin a conversation. You were soaring through the air, higher and higher, daring gravity to hold you back. The swing was meant to hold only the weight of a child, but you had no fear of it giving way under you. No, you knew it would support your body, and all the stress you would put it through. My fingernails dug deep into the flesh of my palm, as I feared you would be flung wildly, if the chains were to give way. Yet, you kept going, your golden hair baring the beauty of your face as you raced toward the sun, and hiding it from me as you reversed direction to build up speed, to see if you could reach new limits. When your excitement and laughter found the extreme height you could travel, a childish yell escaped from your perfect body, filling me with the energy you shared. You made me feel alive, like no one had ever been able to do before. I had no choice. Somehow, I had to become a part of your life.

I apologize the first time didn't go well. I had concentrated so much upon you, I had failed to notice there was another already consumed by your attention. As the swing slowed and I began to approach, he rushed to meet your leap from the seat, and buffer your impact with the pavement below. The hug you two shared gouged away at my insides, and my hopes of us leaving together that day were erased. Still, I decided it would not keep us apart forever. It was only a temporary setback. There would be another day.

As you two headed for the parking lot, I increased my pace to reach my car first. Following at a distance, I stayed behind other cars and trucks, so as not to be noticed in his rearview mirror. You have no idea how pleased I was to see you were a person of principles— your morality displayed by only a quick kiss before you headed into your apartment, alone—him driving off while wishing he was still with you, and experiencing the delights your body offered the lucky one you chose.

I hated to stop and call you back. You'd almost reached your door when I shouted out and asked if you could help me. I got out of the car, but kept it between us. I did so to make you more at ease, as you didn't have to get too close to talk, and could enjoy the safety of your comfort zone. Of course, the person I asked about was fictitious. No, there was no "Jennifer" in my life when we spoke—still isn't. My story about my girlfriend leaving her job with a co-worker and being seen heading toward his apartment was adlibbed on the spot. I know, it was very believable—so much so, I began to believe it as it was told. That's why my voice cracked, and a tear ran down my cheek. I wanted to make it real, so you'd believe me and feel some compassion for my miserable situation.

I hoped you'd stand and talk a while, perhaps, gaining an interest in one whose love was spurned for another. I continued about how I only wanted to make her happy by doing the little things, like taking long walks together, going to the park and acting as if we were children upon the swings and merry-go-round, and getting ice cream. It was all in hopes you'd see I was perfect for you—the person you wanted to be with forever.

You failed to feel my sorrow. Instead, you acted as though getting away was your quest. So, I let you go without pushing further. I could sense your relief you as you walked away. I apologize for not trying harder. Maybe, if I had, we would have gotten together a more amiable way.

Your parking lot was a great place to sit and fantasize about our life together. Knowing you were upstairs, doing whatever it is you do, was a great comfort to me. I didn't have to worry about you getting attacked by some mugger or rapist, nor did I need fear you making love to another. No, you were all alone, secure behind locked doors, not a care in the world. You may have been making a wonderful meal with which to surprise me, or making sure your make-up was perfect so as not to disappoint when I see you. You may even have been lying on the bed imagining our bodies working together to bring about new heights of sensuality. I wanted you to stay there, next to me, knowing we could do it again if you wished. Afterward, we could lie together in each other's arms, gathering our strength for another go at it later. Pleasing you was all that was ever on my mind.

I was surprised the next weekend when you were picked up by one I hadn't seen before. You two drove off in his big pick-up truck after a quick kiss, as if you'd been with him before. The way he moved his head and arms around as you two talked, indicated him to either be extremely obnoxious, or angered. It worried me. I waited outside the bar for your date to end, ducking down in my seat to avoid the police cruising through from time to time. They weren't needed. I was there to protect you. Lucky I was. He didn't seem too friendly when you both walked out. I saw him try to get you into the rear seat of the truck cab, as if he thought you willing to give him all he wanted. My hand was on the doorknob when you fought him off and stormed down the street. Then, he drove away in the other direction. I couldn't believe he just left you there, walking alone, in that section of town.

You made my life easy when you accepted my invitation to give you a ride home. I knew you trusted me. I'd given you no reason not to do so. Of course, asking if you needed me to call someone to come and get you first helped to put you at ease, especially after the way the other guy had treated you. And, when I asked you if you'd like to have some coffee and give yourself a chance to calm down at my place, I was a little surprised at how quickly you accepted the invitation. I had no idea you were so naïve. You didn't even notice me crushing a couple of sleeping pills and mixing them into the brew. I was amazed.

Things kind of went sour from there, didn't they? You didn't like the room in the basement I'd prepared for you. I never imagined you to be so hard to please. You had all the conveniences, without any of life's problems, there. I even took special care when preparing your meals, to ensure they were exceptionally tasty. I found you loved to scream for no reason. If I had chained you down or tried to force myself upon you, I could have understood, but I did neither. All I had to do was unlock your door, and you started yelling at the top of your lungs. That's the reason I didn't feed you for a couple of days. I figured if you were hungry enough, you would grab the food I offered, instead of yelling. Funny how that worked, isn't it?

I thought if we spent time together, we could begin to appreciate what the other had to offer. You had beauty and energy in abundance, but little intelligence, unfortunately. I was shocked to find that out, having imagined you to be the total package. There was little to no compassion shown by you, either. That was sad to me, as I thought you as one to give others the love they needed, in hopes of receiving the love you required back. It just wasn't there, not even a little bit. You were very demanding and angry all the time, not submissive in the least.

I was somewhat intimidated by those traits. True love requires each to give a little, and learn how to compromise. Your tenacity to fight whatever I suggested became too much of a battle for me to endure. I sought peace and tranquility, with a mate who treasured me as I did her. You proved yourself inadequate to understand or care about my needs, in the least. No, you were too selfish for my liking.

Sitting here, staring into your eyes. I almost wish they could blink, to show some sort of life. Yes, I know it's a dream. No one comes back from being strangled. Funny, but the turtleneck sweater I put on you covers the bruises well. When I wrapped the speaker wire around your neck, you acted as if you hadn't expected me to kill you. Your mouth opened, as if to protest, but there was no air able to escape to enunciate. Sorry, but I never did learn how to read lips. Your face turned a beautiful shade of deep pink and I giggled, knowing that supporting breast cancer research was the least of your concerns. It took much longer to strangle you than expected—almost three minutes. You fought hard to stop me. You really did love life, didn't you?

You'll be happy to know I have seen another who matches ... actually, she surpasses your external beauty, and seems to put your inner beauty to shame. We have talked a few times, usually about the dog she walks every day at the park, and we are beginning to become good friends. Of course, that means I'll be needing this room before long. I hate to have to move you out, but you'd just be in the way.

After all, you and I just didn't mesh well. I'll be taking you out to the woods in a day or two for a nice burial. I'm sorry I can't invite your family, but I'm sure you understand the reasoning behind my reluctance to do so. I'm simply not a people person. No, I'm a one-on-one type—its where my comfort zone lies. So, let's just sit here and enjoy the time we have left with one another. It really is a shame we couldn't make it work ... together.

Landlords

There is warmth in basking in the morning sun, especially for those who fear the darkness of night. They believe it brings an end to the lurking unknown, by illuminating where they hide. With no worry as to where they may lie in wait, confidence rises, and their internal fortitude falsely magnifies itself tenfold. This fake sense of security makes them fools. Evil does thrive in the hours most close their eyes in the land of dreams, but nightmares exist, even as the sun's rays shine. It is ever-present.

This evening, evil laid its clammy fingers upon me and took hold of my reason. I wore the blinders of hate and despair, frustration, and anger, and only when it released its grasp did my true vision return. Twas a sight I wished not to bear witness.

The roof is creaking as it contracts in the coolness, reviving the Earth as the heat of the sun's rays depart. It is as if the house is alive, drawing up into a protective state, fortifying itself against the creatures of the night—hoping they'll pass by for another less prepared. The house is of the same belief as many humans, yet, its actions are much too late. The enemy is already inside.

A kitchen faucet, quiet during the day, relaxes and allows water to seep out. Its steady dripping matches the rhythm of my heart—never slowing down or speeding up—only the steady beat of madness, pounding deep within my chest. I acknowledge its presence and open the doors to my subconscious, as the pumping blood seeks to explode the walls of the tunnels in which it runs wild. The madness rushes, with the force of mighty rapids, to destroy any obstruction and laugh at the fallen it leaves behind. I cannot control the intensity of either the madness or heart—they have lives of their own.

I realize only the physical violence has ceased to continue, as the others rage on. There is grief in what I have done. My remorse arrives, yet, it is scorned by the madness in command.

My mind flips through my memories, as if they are being shuffled like a deck of cards. The face card reminds me children can be assets or liabilities to one's future, dependent on how they are raised and conditioned. Yet, to discover which, they must be allowed to reach adulthood. Elimination of that opportunity is the greatest of sins.

The house had been constructed, with care and precision, in 1937. Its owners hadn't been able to afford a mansion, yet the home exhibited the character and design one would expect in a house more expensive. It had seen many faces over the decades, the last four as a home for the elderly to spend their final years. It served the purpose of providing the perfect site for memories to thrive ... memories of better years passed by ... some reminders of the glory of their youth. If one listened closely, one could hear it moan with the sadness of knowing many of its occupants left no longer breathing. The weight of that sorrow grew when the home was closed, its residents sent to newer, more modern facilities. Empty, the energy of life within dwindled, and its age began to show. The realtors showed it often, but noses snubbed their recommendations. Soon, hoping to recoup some of their investment, they put the home up for rent.

The joys of youth, and the energy of children romping about, should have invigorated the home, making it open its doors in jubilant welcome. Yet, it held onto its ominous appearance, filling the eyes of the children with dread as they clung to their mother's side. It was nothing like their last home. No, this one had a porch railing missing several spokes, flaking paint seeking escape from the weather-beaten wood that lied beneath, and stairs that creaked under the least little weight, as if they were in pain. Along with the dead shrubbery, drying patches of grass, and dark storm clouds above, the home's welcome was more a warning to depart, and not return.

After a week, the initial feelings shared by the sisters had not changed. Alicia and Lynn hated the house. "This place is a dump," "It's not as nice as our old home," "Careful, I bet there are spiders all over the place," and many others, openly carried the tone of their discontent. Even after all the boxes were unpacked and they were settled in, Alicia, the youngest, was heard asking her sister, "Why did Daddy have to die? He never would have made us live here like Mommy does."

Laura did everything possible to help occupy their time and make them happy. At a time when they should have been growing closer, the gap was growing.

"What do you mean, you don't want to kiss me goodnight?"

"Mrs. Evanheart told me that if you loved us, we wouldn't have moved out of our other house and ended up here," Alicia spat out, jerking her head away. "She said that you'd have found a way to keep us in our own home."

"Who is this Mrs. Evanheart?" Laura replied, doing her best to hold back her temper. "Where did you talk to her?" Things had been wearing enough, since her husband's car accident. She had dealt, not only with her own emptiness, but that growing in her children. Larry's long stay in the hospital, in a coma, and then his death, had left the family penniless.

She remembered her shock at finding out Larry's employer had stopped paying the insurance premiums during her husband's coma. She'd been told if he didn't show for work, then they didn't have to pay a thing. Of course, the insurance company had terminated his health insurance because of non-payment. A lawyer had been able to get her a small settlement, but it was only enough to keep the hospital's collection agency off her back for a while. With their house payments far behind, she had no option but to find a cheaper place for her and the girls to live, and let the bank take the house.

Of course, neither of the girls could understand all the things she'd been through, and was still facing. They expected her to be a "home" mom, not a working mother. She'd been stressed at leaving them during the day, dealing with the bank, and finding someplace they could afford in which to live. Her nerves were growing thin. The last thing she needed was some busybody meddling with her children's feelings and making things worse.

"She's a friend of mine that understands me," Alicia whispered, a solitary tear running down her cheek. "She's not like you. She loves me."

"I don't want to kiss you, either," Lynn spoke out, echoing Alicia's resentment. "Mr. Harrison says that if we don't want to live here, that we should move. He said you're only keeping us here because Daddy's not around any longer and you don't, and never did, care about what we want. You're only thinking of yourself."

"Who is this Mrs. Evanheart and Mr. Harrison?" Her voice couldn't restrain the anger flowing. "I want to know, and I want to know, now!"

Both girls turned on their sides, with their backs to her, and pulled the covers over their heads.

"All right, if that's the way you want to be, neither of you are going outside until you tell me. Besides coming downstairs to eat your meals, and going to the bathroom, you're restricted to your room. We'll see how much you hate it here." Laura jumped up and stormed to the bedroom door. "Maybe that will make you tell me who these damn people are!"

Slamming the door behind her, she stomped off to her bedroom and threw herself on the bed. How dare the girls refuse to give her a goodnight kiss! All she did for them, and that was their gratitude. Were they really the spoiled brats they were acting like?

Something was happening to her. Instead of shedding her normal quantity of self-pity tears, she began to get bitter ... so bitter she wanted to hurt someone. Not someone, she wanted to hurt the girls. All her frustrations came to the surface. The ceiling disappeared and a vision of her holding a belt in her hand appeared. Made of thick leather and brandishing a huge brass buckle, it felt natural doubled up in her hand. Her daughters lay in their beds in front of her, the covers pulled down to their ankles. Standing between them, she first swung the belt down on Alicia's butt, with all her might, and then turned and did the same to Lynn's. Back and forth, she slammed the belt upon their bodies. Both girls cowered in a fetal position, screaming in pain as she kept swinging her weapon. She found their cries amusing, and broke out in laughter as she noticed strips of blood and raw flesh clinging to the leather.

Waking up, Laura was horrified at what she'd dreamt. Bursting into tears, she clung tightly to her pillow and prayed for God to help her keep her sanity. Then, she wept some more.

For the next two weeks, the sisters appeared to be content to stay in their room. They spoke only when spoken to outside its confines, and returned voluntarily, without a word from their mother. Their refusals to describe who the two mysterious friends were, and where they talked, only created more conflict within the home. Their heads, filled with resentment and new-found hatred, created a barrier Laura couldn't break through.

The hostile atmosphere was anything but conducive to what they'd had when Larry had been living. Laura never imagined life without him, but now she had to experience it, and she didn't like what she found. All the problems were getting to her, and destroying her hopes of the girls ever rekindling their love for her ... and she them. The money was almost gone. Soon, they wouldn't be able to afford to pay the rent. Social services would take the girls away, and she'd be alone, unless she could come up with some sort of job to pay the bills. Losing the girls would almost be a good thing. Maybe they'd find parents they loved, instead of one they seemed to despise.

Taking a swig of coffee, its bitterness made Laura grimace. She'd made better pots. It was as if everything she'd attempted to do since moving into the old home had been a failure. Maybe the girls were right in hating the house. It wasn't as if there had been any other choices at the time, and now, with money running out, the options were even less.

The weight of the world sat on her shoulders … and she physically felt it there. Trying to reach for her coffee cup, her body refused to respond. Laura's head began to swim, much like when she'd had her vision of beating the girls a few days before. Leaning her head back against the couch cushions, her thoughts turned to alternatives … ways for her to alleviate her worries. *If the girls were gone, I'd be free. No longer would the shackles of being a responsible parent be mine. Life. and all it had to offer, would be mine for the taking. I could be young again, party all night, and travel the world. I could even find another man … a rich one, this time. No more dealing with hate and resentment, only happiness. I could achieve that without the girls. It would be easy. I could take the girls swimming at the lake and dare them to swim across. I'd make fun of them until they accepted, and be too slow to swim out and save them when they failed. I could play the part of a grieving mother and find sympathy from the community. First, losing my husband, and then the girls, everyone would take me into their homes out of goodwill—they might even introduce me to their male friends. I'd have my life back!*

There had been no tears when she'd awakened and found herself able to move normally once again. No remorse over her thoughts. The millstone around her neck was about to be removed. It was amazing how much better her coffee tasted.

The girls had been excited about the trip to the lake. The weather forecast had predicted a warm and sunny afternoon. Laura had practiced looking distressed and frantic in her bedroom mirror. Everything was set for the perfect "accident" to tragically take place.

Predicting the weather has never been a guarantee.

Rain ... not drops, but sheets of rain ... filled the street with inches of flowing water.

Laura stared out her living room window, watching the downpour drench the neighborhood. Her hopes, now dashed for at least one day, took her to the three-way intersection of Anger, Frustration, and Remorse, with the bypass of Guilt circling them all. Surprisingly, there was no disappointment in having to delay her plans. After all, the girls were of her body. They had been nursed by her, comforted by her, and cared for by her, for years. How could she throw all of that away?

The girls were watching television at the other end of the room. She'd ended their restriction to their room, but after a few minutes, both had rose and gone back to their previous prison. A pronounced closing of their bedroom door announced their preference. They had no need for her, or television. Laura had been excluded from their life.

Leaving her window seat, Laura grabbed her glass and headed to the kitchen. The lightheadedness she had previously felt took hold, causing her to stumble forward. Reaching out, Laura's fingers found the counter and gave her a place to steady herself. The darkness taking control, her thoughts ran wild. *How dare those little bitches! I try to be nice and they pull this shit. If they don't want to be around me, well, I don't want to be around them. Such insolence ... they need to be taught a lesson. They need to be taught a lesson. Not with my hand, either. No, it's time to bring the belt out!*

The image of an old leather strap hanging in the basement came to mind. No, wait, that wouldn't be enough. Next to it hung an old metal chain ... possibly from a bicycle ... that would be perfect. The metal links would create a much more severe impact against their bodies. It was what they needed ... something to teach a lesson ... something to show them to have respect for their mother ... something to free up her life.

Without hesitation, down the basement steps she hurried. The chain hung just as remembered. Its metal links were cold in her hand ... cold and so very hard. Swinging it against her calf, tremendous pain shot through her body and she fell to the floor. Moaning, she rubbed her leg for several minutes until the pain began to subside. Yes, there would be a bruise—but the children would have many!

Using the light from the open door to ascend the stairs, she rushed to the top in seconds. Through the doorway came one of the heavy wooden kitchen chairs, one of its legs slamming into her forehead. She fought against losing consciousness, dropping the chain and scrambling to find the banister, until her mind cleared. Again, the chair leg slammed against her forehead. Falling backward, her feet found only air awaiting, but her body hit stair after stair as it bounced to the concrete floor at the bottom.

Setting down the chair, the girls watched the body below as they descended into the basement. For several minutes, they sat on the bottom step and searched for any sign of movement from their mother's body. Satisfied their work was done, they smiled at each other and started back up to the kitchen.

Simultaneously, both were grabbed by their shoulder-length hair and yanked backward. Arms flailing, they hit the cement and lay there, stunned. In their eyes, their mother hovered above, no worry about their condition or injuries present. Kneeling, Laura first took hold of Alicia's head and slammed it back against the floor. The sound of a skull cracking echoed against the thunder of the storm outside. Turning to Lynn, she repeated her act, not once, but twice, before doing the same to Alicia.

Before her, two young bodies lie still. No breathing, no heart pumping, all bodily functions ceased. Only the spreading of the pools of blood beneath each head provided any change to the scene, over the time Laura gazed at them. They seemed so innocent lying there, side by side, no anger or hate present, only peace. She wondered what had changed them into what they'd become, upon entering the house. What had changed her?

At the top of the stairs, the chain she'd dropped rose and formed a noose. Wrapping the free end around the banister support, unseen hands stretched it out until the noose was directly above Laura's head. In an instant, the noose found its place around her throat.

Laura's fingers clawed away at the chain, but found it too tight to get a grip on. Her feet were pulled out from under her, and she found herself being drug away, the chain digging in deeper as the force of many pulled her toward the outside wall. She tried to scream, but the links embedded in her throat only allowed a raspy growl to emerge. It wasn't long before she no longer struggled, her body lying as still as the two beside it.

I congratulated Mrs. Evanheart and Mr. Harrison on their plan. They'd played an intricate part in getting the girls to listen to them. Mr. Foley, the original owner of the house, let out a laugh and thanked all of us for our help. He'd taken on the responsibility of handling the mother's phases into the darkness, and been perfect in his efforts.

See, if you don't want to live here, then move. We've been here for many, many decades and love it. In fact, we plan on staying forever. The last thing we want are people living here complaining about our home. We'll get you out ... one way or another.

That's just the way it is.

Blessed?

Her sails full of salt air, the grand lady approached the pier at breakneck speed. Her journey, long and filled with unexpected obstacles, had both passengers and crew praying for a rest from the rhythm of the sea. Too many days of constant rocking with the choppy waves, sleepless nights in swaying hammocks, and tin dishware sliding across the tables at each meal, had been the price they'd paid to arrive at their destination. In addition, the violent storms they'd encountered had extended their journey by over a week. Supplies had run low, and fear of ending up at the bottom of Davy Jones' Locker forever had taken its toll on their sanity. No wonder the dash down the gangway to solid ground resembled a mad scramble, instead of the expected standard debarkation.

Word of her pending arrival had traveled fast. The crowd, filled with distinguished gentlemen in top hats and suits and ladies in hoop skirts, filled the greeting area with an array of color and glitz, in accordance with their high position in society in the new century of 1800. Even an orchestra had been quickly assembled, and played in perfect unison, with only enough volume to be a minor distraction to conversation during the occasion.

Many of those leaving the vessel immediately took advantage of the vendors along the streets, and the treats they offered. Days without fresh fruits and candies found plenty of customers craving their offerings, among those with limited budgets, as did the shops behind them catering to the wealthier crowd. The intensity of their departure from the sea, and relief at being back to civilization, depleted pocket cash and filled stomachs, as food items were devoured. There seemed to be something for everyone.

Even those who cared not about life's little pleasures.

Most of my money had been gambled away in the rigged card games during our trip. I should have known better, but the boredom of the moment had driven me to indulge. My stomach growled for a food item not covered in the gray mold of that onboard, but with limited funds, my choices were slim. Regrettably, I forfeited several of my cherished personal items from my bag, as I bartered for a meal. I missed them not, as each bite of the bowl of hot stew and loaf of fresh bread was savored. I left no drop or crumb, licking the bowl clean upon finishing. My immediate needs satisfied, I pulled the last of my tobacco from its pouch patted it into my pipe. Sitting there with a full stomach and smoking pipe, I found time to be grateful. Life was good … for the moment.

With the day's light fading and recognizing a chill to the air, I concentrated my efforts on my next need—a safe place to lay my body down for a night's rest. The few coins left in my pocket would not afford me a bed, so I roamed the streets, looking for a suitable place out of the cold sea breezes, and the views of pedestrians and police. My hopes were to find a job of some sort the next day, get paid, buy back the items I had traded for the meal, and find proper accommodations within a few days. Until then, I would join the street people, and do my best to survive.

I passed an alley and backed up to give it a better look. It was filled with various items that had been tossed out, probably by some landlord who had emptied the apartment of one he had evicted. I entered and made my home behind a trash bin. A stained feather mattress would serve as my bed, and a set of ragged curtains as my blanket. Most of the night breeze was blocked, so I should be able to survive until morning, without fear of being found frozen stiff. I settled down and lie there thinking about what the future might hold, hoping sleep would find me shortly.

"Hello, stranger. My name is Michael. Who you be?"

I jumped, startled at the thought of being helpless while lying on my back. Searching the darkness for the voice's source, I hoped to bluff and threatened, "I mean you no harm, but will defend myself. I warn you ... I'm armed!"

"Now, don't go getting all riled up. I just like to know who I'm sleeping across from. I'm not here to do anything but sleep tonight, and wake up in the morning. You just get off the ship?"

The voice was one of an older man, possibly elderly. Its tone seemed to be friendly enough. I decided to take a chance and talk to him, in hopes of keeping my neck from being sliced as I slept. "Sorry, old man, you

118

surprised me. I didn't see anyone when I set up my sleeping quarters. Yeah, I'm fresh off the ship, as you say. No need to try to shake hands. I can't see you well enough, and would probably trip over something trying to get to you."

"Just as well," he responded, sounding as if he was relieved I was going to stay where I was at. "I'm already warm and want to keep it that way. Tonight's wind is cold enough to cut you in half. Won't be that way long. Summer's almost here. But, enough talk, I worked all day and am tired. Didn't make much money, only enough to fill my stomach. Some days are like that. Others are better. Don't really need much. Wife is dead, so there's only me to worry about."

"Sorry to hear that," I said, hoping to show some empathy for his plight. Then again, mine wasn't much better. "Are there many jobs available around here?"

"Not many ... not that pay enough to live on. That's why I carve things out of wood. I can grab a scrap board and make something people will like. Makes them and me both happy. I'm pretty good with my knives, if I do say so myself. Enough talk, I need my sleep. You stay over there, and I'll stay here. Like you warned me, I'll do the same to you. I want us both to wake up in the morning."

The sight of the morning sky shed all doubts he'd kept his word.

Across the alley, there was no hint anyone had slept there. He had either cleaned up well after himself, or had been a figment of my imagination. Either way, he was gone, and I was alive. To me, that was all that mattered.

Hiding the mattress and curtains under some boards—in case I had to return there again—I headed off to seek out employment. Yet, I discovered most were not concerned about my desires to find a position. Instead, the conversation of the day was one of concern and fear. Although death was a common occurrence in the city, it was rare for an entire family be struck down, in the safety of their own home. Disease, although dreaded, would have been less eventful than the violent death they had all received by a knife, in the hand of a murderer.

None could understand it. The police had made a statement earlier, and requested anyone with any information come forward. I learned robbery was not the reason, as cash was left behind in plain view. All had been stabbed several times and decapitated, even the young children. People were upset, afraid, and angered at the senseless killings, all at once.

Needless to say, the news didn't help my chances of finding a position. I would go hungry until I could either find one, or be lucky enough to benefit from someone's charity. With the number of beggars lining the streets, starvation seemed the most likely. Over and over, I was turned away. No one seemed to care about all I could do. They didn't have a position available, and that was it. As the day's end grew close, a shopkeeper took pity upon my plight. He told me about his brother, in need of someone to help him on his farm.

"It doesn't pay much, and the work is hard, but he needs someone to help him. If you really want work, I'll give you the directions to his farm. You'll not make it there tonight, but if you'll leave in the morning, you can walk there before the sun goes down."

He even threw in a stale loaf of bread that had started to mold. It was better than going hungry.

I returned to the alley and spent another cold night. This time, there was no one with me. I suspected the old man had made enough money selling his carvings to spend the night in a real bed. I was jealous at knowing him warm and comfortable, while I was fighting a devious wind that never gave up trying to freeze me solid. It was no problem to begin my journey to the man's farm at daybreak. Walking was the only way I could warm up.

Following the directions I'd been given, I shuffled along at a steady pace. Passing several streams along the way, I drank to sate my thirst and quiet the noises my empty stomach was making. By mid-afternoon, I'd reached the place matching the description the shopkeeper had given. First trying the house, I received no answer to my knocking. Hearing a commotion out by the barn, I chose my way carefully through the weeds, avoiding the areas of briars scattered about. Almost there, I hollered out "Hello" several times. Last thing I wanted was to surprise, and find a musket ball my reward.

"Who be there?" came a voice from around the corner of the barn. "Better not be a peddler. Don't need anything. Got all I need. Best to be on your way."

Turning the corner, a muscular man in his forties stood firm. His face showed the years of working the farm by himself, in every crack and wrinkle. He presented the image of a soldier who had fought too many battles and been put out to pasture by the generals who couldn't control him. The huge blade in his hand still had shreds of the leather strips along the fence he had been trimming, but was now readied for any assault that might be made.

"I'm from the city. Your brother told me you needed help. I hope that's the case. I'm tired of sleeping in an alley, haven't eaten in two days, and am dead broke. You don't need that knife, unless you're planning on cutting up one of those cows I saw out in the pasture. I could probably eat the whole thing."

You have no idea how relieved I was when his mouth formed a smile and the blade was hung upon the fence post.

"Been a long time since I had any help. Could have used you a week ago. I repair and make harnesses for the farmers around here. Got so much work scheduled, I can't take care of the farm properly. So, I need someone to help me out in both areas. Work won't be easy, and I can't pay much, but you'll have three meals a day and a place to sleep, out in the barn. Still interested?"

Six months later, we almost had the farm in shape. I'd gained his trust by doing exactly as he asked, never veering off and ignoring his instructions. It was his farm, so it was his right to have things done as he wanted. Doing so gained his favor. He even went out and bought a pot-bellied stove for the barn, to keep me warm during the coming winter weather.

Summer's end meant a slowdown to the work. I'd saved every penny I'd earned, and asked him for a few days off. I'd traded off my father's pocket watch and my mother's picture in an ornate frame, the first day we hit port, in order to eat. I wanted them back. Now, since I had money, I could go back and hopefully find them. I figured I'd have to pay twice as much to get them back, but it would be worth it. He was amiable to the idea and told me not to take too long, or he might have to hire someone to take my place, and then laughed. As well as we had hit it off, I knew he was only joking.

Instead of having to walk to the city, I was able to take one of the farmer's horses. The miles passed much faster than during the original trip, even stopping an hour to rest the horse and allow her to drink from one of the streams. I reached the outskirts of the city by late morning, and found a stable to house the horse while I began my search.

Luck was with me, as my mother's picture was found almost immediately. I was able to purchase it back for the same amount I'd received months before. My father's watch was a much different story. I was able to locate it, and offered an amount over what I'd been paid, but the vendor demanded an outrageous sum, regardless of the amount he had given me. Our voices increased in volume as tempers began to flare, drawing a large crowd. Most of those screamed for him to stop being a horse's ass and cut his price to what he'd given. Soon, a constable arrived and stated the vendor could charge what he wanted for the item. Boos rang out from the crowd. Completely unexpected, a young man rushed in, snatched the watch from the cart, and ran off, the policeman following. The crowd cheered, thinking the vendor had received justice for trying to cheat me. I wasn't as happy. My father's watch was gone.

Saddened, I found lodging for the night and took my sorrow to a pub. A meal and drink consumed, I headed to my room for a night of rest. I wanted to head back to the farm early the next morning, so I planned on retiring early. Before I could dim the lantern, a knock came from the door.

I opened it and found the constable from the vendor's cart waiting. A smile came to his face upon seeing me. "I've been looking for you for hours. I have something you might want."

Lifting his arm, my father's pocket watch dangled from his fingers. Taking it from him, the sadness I'd felt earlier was only a forgotten memory.

"I've dealt with that crook before," he spoke out with authority. "When I saw you dealing with him, I knew you had no chance of bartering him down. The bastard would rather sell later to someone at a lower price, than have a crowd hear him lower the asking price. So, I asked one of the lads I know to grab it and run, something he's done well on his own in the past. I gave him a couple of shillings for doing so. I'd appreciate getting those back, but nothing more. Getting the better of the vendor is enough satisfaction."

I thanked the man and handed him the shillings he had requested. I lay back on the bed and stared at the watch. I'd never expected to get it back after the day's events, and here it was. Between the job at the farm, and being able to once again own my mother's picture and my father's watch, I was truly blessed.

I woke, splashed some water on my face, and left my room the next morning. Stopping downstairs for a quick pastry and a cup of tea, I overheard conversations not unlike those I'd heard prior to leaving the city before. Another family had been murdered, in the same manner as the last. Most had believed the killer to have moved on, as there had been none during the time of my absence. I kept quiet and took it in. To have done otherwise would only have cast suspicion upon myself.

The smell of the city, though rancid in areas, brought back many happy memories. I'd been raised in a city, much like this one. I changed my route and walked along the waterfront, recalling my younger years, when the other boys and I fished. Seldom did we catch anything, but the stories we told and the antics we got into kept our parents and the local authorities on their toes.

As I came to a pile of boulders along the shoreline, a figure came into view. It was an old man, sitting off to himself, carving a toy ship out of a piece of driftwood. He was humming an old song, one of the seas and the maidens left behind, his voice very familiar.

"I remember sleeping in an alley one night with a gentleman stating he was a carver of things that made people happy," I spoke out, watching to see if there was any reaction to my words. "I spent most of the night wondering if he was going to carve me, instead."

"Aye, and I spent the night wondering if the man across the way thought me ignorant enough to believe he was armed with a pistol."

We both broke out in laughter.

Rising to his feet, he stuck out his hand in friendship. "I saw you last night at the pub and remembered that evening. You were still asleep the next morning, when I had to decide whether to kill you or let you live. I decided if you had anything worth robbing you for, you wouldn't be sleeping in an alley. I knew you hadn't seen my face in the dark that cold evening, so I let ye be, last night. Now, you're here, and we're talking as if we've known each other forever. The Lord works in strange ways, my friend, strange ways, indeed."

For over an hour, we discussed the last few months. He'd been doing as always, making money some days, and none on others. He was very interested in where I'd gone, and what I had been doing. I filled him in on all that had happened, and gave him directions to the farm and invited him to stop by should he ever decide to take a vacation from the city. At first, I balked at his invitation to share an evening meal together, as the shillings I'd given the constable had depleted my pockets of any money. He told me he had some extra saved and would make a strong effort to sell something later, to have enough for both of us to have a full stomach. I hesitated, hating to empty his pockets for a meal, but agreed, at his insistence.

The farm was waiting, and my plans didn't include staying away another day. Yet, a chance to enjoy some of the comforts the city offered was too much of a temptation to deny myself. I walked the streets for the remainder of the afternoon, partaking of the sights and sounds. Unlike the silence surrounding me in the country, here one could feel the energy flowing through their body. So many people talking, carriages and carts rumbling along the cobblestone streets, even the laughter of the children playing—all provided a joy for my soul. I began to long to be a constant part of the activity, instead of being a kind of hermit, so far away from it, at the farm. Yes, I would come back here to live in the future. I would stay with the farmer for a few more months, save my money as before, and then return to locate employment.

Dusk came almost too soon, but the music coming from the various eating and drinking establishments brought a smile to my face. I stood outside the pub I'd visited the previous night, awaiting the arrival of my friend, Michael. The growling of my stomach at the smell of the offerings inside created an impatience, as he failed to show at the designated time. Another hour passed, and then another—still no Michael.

As a late hour approached, I gave up my hopes of sating the hunger, and accepted the fact he wasn't going to show. I wondered if he'd met with some sort of accident or illness. Perhaps he had sliced his hand or arm while carving, and was being cared for by a physician. Had he been robbed of his funds en route to meet me, and killed by one more desperate? What if he was embarrassed to show, as he'd sold nothing and couldn't come up with the money to meet his promise to pay? Or, had the old man's memory failed him and he was wandering about? None mattered. I had neglected to go back to the farm where my evening would be spent in the safety of the barn, with my stomach full, and now must find a place to spend the evening. Unsure if it be chance or fate, I found myself back at the alley in which we'd first met. As expected, the mattress I'd stored had been taken by another. I grabbed a few loose boards to sit upon and spent the night less than comfortably.

When morning came, I returned to the stable where I had housed the farmer's horse. I was reminded by the blacksmith I'd only paid for one night, not two, and needed to come up with the difference before I could leave. Pockets empty, I noticed several harnesses lying across the top of a stall and, after informing him of my skills, inquired if my repairing them would satisfy the bill. He agreed. I made quick work of them, as my experience with the farmer had given me skills not found among city dwellers. While working, I spoke to the man of my desire to return to the city to live. Not only did my efforts satisfy my debt, but the blacksmith provided me a hearty lunch, and offered a permanent position working at the stable. He agreed to allow me a month or two to ensure the farmer would not be left unable to fill his current commitments before starting, but wanted my promise to return at that time. I happily gave it.

With my future assured, I mounted my mare and headed back to the farm. I thought of the farmer and how grateful I needed to be for the skills he had shared. We had become friends, and I would be sad to leave him, but the life the city offered was too much to my liking. I debated upon telling him my news immediately, or delaying it. My return to the city would be a cold one, as I was sure to be walking instead of riding his horse there, and the weather would soon turn. I felt I owed him some time to prepare for my departure, but didn't want to delay too long, as walking the distance in snowdrifts was far from my wishes. I hoped he would understand, and we could remain friends. His was a bridge I didn't want to burn, in case the city position turned out to be less than promised.

It was late when I saw the silhouette of the barn ahead. The farmhouse was already dark, illuminated only by the moon and stars. Not wanting to awaken the farmer, I quietly entered the barn and shed the horse of the saddle and harness. A grain sack over her mouth, she stood still as I attended to wiping her down and brushing the remnants of our journey from her coat. Finished, I noticed the other animals had not been fed. Taking care of their needs, I wondered why they had been ignored. Surely the farmer hadn't forgotten them. Could he be ill or injured, and awaiting assistance inside the house?

I trod out the barn door and smelled the air. Normally, the smell of smoldering wood from his pot-bellied stove would fill the air. With no breeze to send it another direction, there was no hint of a fire ever having been lit. I knocked at his front door, gently at first, and then louder as my rapping went unanswered. I chanced his anger and stuck my head in his door, yelling out to him as I did so. Again, no response. Gathering up my courage, I took a step inside, almost slipping on something wet under my boot. It clung to my foot as I tried to take another step, wanting to hold me prisoner. I took out a match and struck it. My eyes wished I hadn't.

Lying on the floor was the farmer, his upper body covered in blood. I leaned over with the match in front of me, to see more clearly. The blood came not only from multiple stab wounds in his chest, but from a deep slice across his throat, extending almost from ear to ear. Beside him, a musket lay, its ammunition shot, but no sign of its target being struck anywhere.

He was beyond help. It had obviously been hours since breath had exited his body.

Feeling the sting of the fire reach my fingers, I dropped the match and heard it sizzle as it dimmed in the blood covering the floor. I stood, in the darkness, wondering if the murderer was still on the premises, or had departed before my arrival. Hoping I was alone, I left the house and returned to the barn. I searched to ensure I was alone there, not wanting to end up as the farmer. Grabbing a knife and a pitchfork, I huddled behind some wooden crates and wondered what I should do next.

Everything told me to run, to go back to the city and pretend I'd never returned. Yet, I couldn't—not and make sure the farmer had a proper burial. He had been too kind to me to allow his body to rot and be eaten away at by the field mice and rats. The sunrise was several hours away. I would mount the mare and ride to the local constable's office first thing, reporting what I'd found. To do so in the night would be ignorant, chancing attack by one of the night creatures along the way. I had no desire to meet my maker after having been ripped apart by a pack of wolves. No, morning would be soon enough.

The questions were answered over and over, the same way, but the constable seemed less than convinced. He believed I had returned and gotten into an argument with the farmer. Tempers flaring, I supposedly grabbed a knife and did the deed. Only recognizing the depth of my attack when it had ended, I then made up the story and waited until morning to report it. I sat in the cell until the time of my departure had been confirmed by the blacksmith in the city. The state of the body demonstrated that I had not had the time to do the deed, but still, the suspicions lingered. Unknown to me, the farmer had inquired as to what would be necessary in order to leave the farm to me, upon his death. Our friendship had been greater than ever imagined, but now, worked as a motive to make his death take place sooner than anticipated. This, too, was cast aside, as no papers had been signed to legalize his intentions.

As too many questions about my innocence failed to confirm my guilt, I was released. I was saddened to learn my days incarcerated had kept me from attending the funeral services of the farmer, and in knowing the farm would soon be sold at a public auction. The livestock had already been divided among several other landowners in the area, to ensure they'd be taken care of and not starve, awaiting sale. Thus, I entered a barn void of life, a replica of the emptiness inside the farmhouse sitting beside it. Gathering my few personal items, I left my past home behind and began the long walk back to the city.

The blacksmith was surprised to see me return so soon. He listened to my tale of recent events, and accepted my vow of innocence. I learned him to be a friend of the shopkeeper (the brother of the murdered farmer) and had discussed the killing with him upon his return from the funeral. I was warned to stay away from the shopkeeper, as he felt me guilty of the crime and wanted only vengeance for his brother's death. He appreciated my desire to confront the man and proclaim my innocence, but thought it would prove hazardous to my health, and possibly to the blacksmith's business. After all, who would want to do business with one housing a suspected murderer?

Several weeks passed, and I proved to the blacksmith I was worth the money he paid for my services. He had been purchasing new harnesses much too often, and cutting into his profits. My services not only kept that from taking place, but he was able to offer others my services and make additional income. My living in the stable gave him a person to be present, to accept late evening business, something he'd not had prior. His wife, accompanied sometimes by his eldest daughter, brought us a more than sufficient lunch each day, and sat with us while we ate. New friendships were growing.

One slow afternoon, the blacksmith told me to take a few hours off. I appreciated his offer and headed off to the shops holding so many things I could only dream of owning. A particularly fancy lamp caught hold of my attention, its multi-colored glass shade resembling that of a church's stained-glass window.

"Do you really think that would look right, next to your cot in the stable?"

I spun around and found the blacksmith's daughter, smiling. Embarrassed at being reminded of my status in society and place in life, the heat of my face turning red made me turn away, and shy from giving a response.

"Wait … I was only teasing. Don't go away. I want to talk to you."

I stopped as if ordered to do so. Before I could say a word, she began prattling on about how she'd been interested in finding out more about me for quite some time. It wasn't hard to figure out she had found me somewhat to her liking. I was truly blessed.

We walked and talked for hours, visiting various shops and joking about some of the items we saw, as well as agreeing on several we loved. Time passed much too quickly. With each second, I found myself being attracted to her in ways her father would disapprove. My livelihood in danger, I began to be more careful in the words I spoke. I wanted her to realize I wasn't to be in her future, and there was no reason to pursue that avenue. We found ourselves in a shop I found familiar. Glancing up, my eyes met those of one I'd seen before. This time, the face was not that of kindness, but of anger.

"You have a lot of nerve to show yourself here," roared the voice, as the man came out from behind the counter. "You get away with killing my brother, and now you come here to flaunt it in my face. And, you do so in the company of my friend's daughter! I should kill you right here and now. Leave, I say, leave now before I do so."

Elizabeth's face in shock at his accusations, I left her standing and fled from the establishment in embarrassment. Entering the sidewalk, I slammed into a man, another I recognized. It was Michael. The shopkeeper close behind, I had no time to waste. I struggled to hurry through the crowd and escape his ire.

I told my tale to the blacksmith, upon arriving at the stable. He, none too happy about my actions with his daughter, or with his friend, threatened to release me from my job … to end our commitment together. I begged him to reconsider and promised to stay away from his daughter as well as his friend, the shopkeeper. Still angry, he told me to be careful who I let into the stable that evening and we would discuss our agreement in greater detail in the morning, after he had time to calm down.

All night, I sat in fear of losing my position. Why had I allowed his daughter to carry my emotions away? Had it been so long since I'd had the companionship of a female, I was so desperate as to jeopardize my position? Common sense had left me, and human desires took control. My stupidity was about to cost me all I had worked to achieve, professionally, was well as the loss of a valued friendship. Depression had found a new home.

Morning arrived, as did the blacksmith ... but not alone. With him were two constables who shackled my hands and led me away. Refusing to answer my questions as to what was happening and why, I was tossed into the back of a police wagon and later jailed. Only after hours of sitting alone in the darkness of an underground cell, was I told of the circumstances.

A house maid had escaped being murdered only by running from the home and screaming at the top ·of her lungs for help from next door neighbors. Her story told a tale of her employers being killed by a man she hadn't seen. Two young boys had been sliced open from neck to groin, the mother decapitated, and the father stabbed multiple times in the chest and then sliced from ear to ear. The description of the father's wounds matched two others they had on file, one almost a year before, and the other on an outlying country farm. The attack had been on the family of the shopkeeper that had threatened me. My ties to his threats, and the similarities with the farmer's wounds, brought them to me ... the murderer of both. I learned there were similarities with another family, the first one that had taken place the night before I'd originally left the city. I was to be charged with those murders, as well.

My innocence was denounced at the trial. Although all evidence was circumstantial, I stood and faced a jury announcing they had found me guilty of all crimes. A familiar voice rang out from the rear of the court chamber, "Hang him, Hang him." I recognized it as that of Michael, supposedly my friend. Could he have fallen victim to the words of the prosecutor, and thought me guilty, as well?

Led from the chamber, I experienced the shock of the verdict. I was to die for crimes I had not committed. How could that be? I'd done nothing, and only hearsay had been presented. The fact that I had been in the city, along with thousands of others, had convicted me of the family killings—my employment at the other had done so there. Surely this wasn't happening, yet, taken to my cell, there was no alternative to consider.

Now, I stand high above the crowd, upon the scaffolding constructed, my feet standing upon a door that will soon open. I refuse the bag they wish to put over my head. If I am to hang by the neck, I want all those present to see the face of an innocent man dying. I search the crowd, hoping to find Elizabeth's face, or even those of her parents. They are absent from the jeering mass. Close to the front, I see that of Michael's. His is jeering as well, yet, enjoying the scene in front of him. He pulls a knife from his jacket and runs it in front of his neck, side to side, smiling as he does so. He is mouthing words for me to see. They seem to be, "Shoot me." It makes no sense to me. Why would he say that? He bends down, just before the order to pull the lever is given, and tosses a basket high. It lands at my feet. From inside, rolls Elizabeth's decapitated head.

I scream out as the door beneath me opens and I drop, the heavy rope around my neck tightening. It was Michael, I realize, Michael was the killer and it will be discovered he killed, again! He used me as a scapegoat, and now flaunts it as my neck snaps and I am plunged into darkness.

I will see you again, you bastard. I will refuse entrance into Heaven and see you in Hell. You will pay, I promise, you will pay!

Desert Sales

To a salesperson, there is no greater joy beyond that of closing a sale. The sale doesn't have to be a huge one. Any sale will suffice. The ability to motivate a person into making an intelligent buying decision is not only great for the ego, but it feeds the wallet, as well. There is an art to taking a person who has no intent on making an immediate purchase, and maneuvering them through the proven steps ... an art not everyone can perfect. To do so takes quick wit, practice, and the ability to empathize ... not sympathize. One must "go for the throat" and take no prisoners, by believing the customer has no better option than owning the product they sell. In essence, it's a game where one wins and one loses, although the salesperson always believes it's a "win-win" solution.

Yeah, I'm a salesperson, just like my father was, only better. He peddled insurance policies door-to-door, and managed to keep his family fed. I recall him telling so many stories about visiting all his clients each month to collect their monthly payments—some entertaining, some hilarious—and how many of the meals he partook of were less than edible. (his "cold chitterlings and chilled macaroni and cheese" among the strangest). His eyes would bulge open as he exclaimed, "Even the cockroaches ran away ... fast!"

No, college isn't necessary to be in sales. Most good salespeople make more income than college graduates. Plus, we're not stuck in one place, wasting our lives away behind a desk every day of our lives, either. We're out meeting new contacts and friends, enjoying great conversations and business lunches, and experiencing all life has to offer. Each Monday, I load up the van with the various prototypes we offer, and head out to cover my territory. With it covering a one-hundred-mile radius, I'll never run out of prospects. They're everywhere!

Like most other businesses, the economy "rises and declines" have an effect. Recent political events haven't been a positive, as the stock markets show only too well. As stocks spiral downward, sales follow a similar pattern. Customers get scared and back out of their commitments to purchase, products are returned under the ninety-day trial period clauses, and appointment doors close without warning. Like a roller coaster ride, sometimes you're at the top of the peak, and other times you're struggling to get up the next hill. All a salesperson can do is to keep doing what made them successful, and hope for the best.

Of course, these low periods are when parent companies panic. They rush to premiere a new product—one the customer can't do without—to enhance sales. Thinking their salespersons are part of the sales decline, they offer bonuses for those who can break down the doors of rejection and sell their new offering. If the product doesn't bring in immediate profits, the employees are again to blame, and replacements are interviewed. It's all about the bottom-line profit to them.

The human loyalty element holds no bearing. Sell, and you stay employed. Don't sell, and you're looking for another job.

I left my house Monday morning with a mediocre attitude, and worry about the health of my family. The wife and kids had eaten at a restaurant known for failing health inspections last Friday, and had come down with an intestinal malady over the weekend. I hated to leave them in such a state, but couldn't afford to stay at home. With all the standard bills coming in, I couldn't take a chance on losing my job to the company's quest for "new blood" replacements. Van loaded, I checked in with the office, pulled out of the driveway, and headed down the highway.

In trying times, I found the smaller towns to contain the best prospects. Big city businesses had multiple competitors, all trying to get their piece of the pie. Many times, businesses in smaller towns only had one or two competitors, and were seeking the edge to beat them. Generally, it took many visits to win their trust, but their long-term loyalty was greater, once you did.

My territory included the Four Corners area, where the borders of Arizona, Colorado, New Mexico, and Utah all meet. The surrounding area is low in population, but high in desert. It provided a very peaceful and calming drive to clear the brain of negativity. Classic Rock on the radio and air conditioning cooling the air, real-world problems tended to disappear.

The scenery and highway never changed along the route. Oh, there might be a new pothole, and different roadkill locations, but the ride provided no surprises. The lack of oncoming traffic allowed me to enter my peaceful zone. Besides the quick blur of a passing gas station, or the thud of my tires riding over a rattlesnake taking its last trip across the highway, I relaxed and enjoyed the drive. In a few hours, I'd be at a motor inn, sitting in a swimming pool, cold drink in hand, and listening to the sound of a coyote yapping in the distance. It would be so surreal, and add a mystique to the spiritual side of darkness. When at peace with myself and the world, I would return to my room and ready myself for four days of heavy prospecting and selling.

Or, so I thought.

Three weeks ago, I had put in a request for a new set of tires for the company van. My old tires didn't care, they'd soon be able to retire. One decided it would take early retirement, instead of waiting on the red tape to go through. Standing next to the flat, I looked at the company's decision to save money on spares in my hand … a quick-repair kit. If the decision makers stood where I did, they would regret their decision, as it proved itself to be completely ineffective. I was stranded alongside the highway, as the sun dipped below the horizon and said its goodbyes to the day. As luck would have it, there was no cellphone coverage.

I had to decide if it would be better to stay in the van overnight, or start walking down the road. I had enough gas for the van's heater to keep me warm during the cool desert night, but when morning came, I would face a long walk in the hot sun. With the closest town only ten miles away, I chose the chill over the heat.

Traveling down the pavement, I began to worry about someone discovering the van and stealing all my prototypes. I validated my decision, knowing insurance would cover the losses, and the flat tire was the company's fault, not mine. If they would have just said "Yes" to the new tires, I'd already be at the motor inn, and their merchandise safe and sound.

The light from the full moon gave me enough illumination to see the outline of the highway. The one fear I had was running into rattlesnakes. At night, they head to the pavement to enjoy the last warmth of day, as the sand cools off much faster. Many, like the Western Diamondback, could give you a bite you wouldn't survive, without immediate treatment. I would be able to see the big ones in the moonlight, but smaller ones, just as deadly, would be more difficult to make out. To save battery life, I turned on the flashlight, scanned the road as far as the beam would reach, and then shut it off. Every step I took was increasing the odds of being my last.

Rattlesnakes weren't the only animals to worry about. Coyotes and mountain lions could also be deadly. Plus, there were always the crazies, out driving the roads and looking for someone to torture and kill. I did my best to stay alert, not focus my attention on anything but the highway ahead. The military had taught me fear can be the great destroyer of moving forward, and reaching your goal. Yet, it could be used to give one the edge, and heighten the senses they needed to succeed. It was a tool I hoped to use.

It happened much sooner than expected.

Before me, the buzzing of a snake's rattle demanded my attention. I'd been focusing on heightening my senses and damn near failed to see the son-of-a-bitch right in front of me. It was a big one, coiled and ready to sink its venom-filled fangs in me, should I venture another step into its strike zone. Its head stayed stationary, as its heat-sensing pits provided it vision far beyond that of its eyes. The rattle slowed its buzz, as if to say, "I'll let you go, if you back away. Otherwise, I will be the bringer of death."

Slowly, I inched myself back, and away from the reptile. If mercy was its offer, I would not refuse. The snake grew quiet, yet did not move. It trusted me no more than I trusted it ... a creature of instinct. Giving it a wide berth, I maneuvered myself around it and continued up the road ... much more vigilant in lighting the way with the flashlight.

A few miles from the van, I noticed a flickering tiny light, in the distance. Perhaps I could find assistance, without walking all the way to town. Again, it was a decision of debate. It could save me miles of dangerous walking, but to get to it, I'd have to walk into the desert and travel among the snakes and other creatures, for almost a mile. I shivered, the night air cooling down much lower than anticipated. If those at the light had an operable phone, I could call a tow truck and get out of the cold. I'd be a fool not to try.

The sand was like soft powder under the soles of my shoes. Some type of bird, startled by my approach, burst from the brush, flapping its wings wildly. The sharp squeal of a desert rat being struck by some predator reminded me that I, too, was prey here.

I let my senses dictate the path through this enemy territory. I was the visitor, not the resident. This was the land of animals, not humans. Beside me could be the creature to cause my death. It might be quick, or slow and painful. If I had my choice, I would prefer it be fast. Setting my sights on the light ahead, I shook my head. I was heading to safety. Only my fear was saying otherwise.

I was now able to see the light was a fire, blazing within a circle of rocks. New energy surged within, knowing it was controlled and maintained ... not running wild. There would have to be people present. With the flashlight batteries being drained of power, I moved onward.

Fifty yards away, I could see the flame was much larger than I had believed. Much of it had been hidden by the large boulders surrounding it. There was a soft chanting of male voices from behind the rocks. I wondered if I had come upon some sort of religious group, possibly Satan worshipers. They would not appreciate a stranger barging in on their secret rites. They could tie me up and leave me to die in the desert. I didn't fancy feeling cold-blooded snakes crawling over me, or the razor-sharp teeth of desert dwellers tearing away bites of my flesh while I screamed in agony, no hope of being saved remaining.

Deciding to proceed with caution, I crept forward, keeping to the shadows whenever possible. I needed to observe their ritual, to attempt to understand the level of danger facing me. Shrugging my shoulders, I did my best to cast away my companion—fear—and keep an open mind. I was thinking the worst, instead of using my reasoning and logic.

Reaching a break in the boulders, I peered through, to see what I could. A group of Indians, native Americans if you will, sat with their legs crossed, giving their full attention to the one standing before them. His feathered headdress seemed to seek flight, as the breeze caused its plumage to blow one direction and then the other. Upon his command, they rose and began dancing around the fire, much like a war dance one might see in the old Western movies, but without the steady beat of war drums and such—only the chanting.   It was mesmerizing ... but frightening, as well.

Standing behind the boulders, I was intoxicated by the sounds and movements. Perhaps, the weariness of the long drive, combined with the adrenaline rush of walking in the darkness and the dangers I'd faced, had a bearing on my state of consciousness. Whatever the reason, it was impossible for me to remove myself from watching. If I was imposing upon a secret rite, the spirits were helping me do so. The fire drew me nearer, around to the gap between boulders. Like a gnat attracted to light, I ventured forward.

The faces of three of the participants hovered above me as I came to, lying on my back. I was tied, spread-eagled, my arms raised high above my head and my legs stretched so tight they fought to stay connected to my body. The chill of night etched its way into my bare flesh as I struggled to free myself—naked to the world. In addition to the anger and fear running through me, I was embarrassed of being stripped of my clothing and self-respect.

"It is always a wonder to see the white man become a red man," a soft voice spoke, hypnotic in its tone. "When your clothes have been removed, the shame of the color of your pale skin runs away, leaving the red behind, to face the enemy. Only when the white skins outnumber the red, does it pretend to be brave."

The voice of the one I'd seen leading the others came from behind me. I tried to move, to see his face as he spoke, but was yanked back so the stars were all I saw. "I'm sorry if I did something wrong. I broke down along the highway and needed help. I saw your fire and hoped to find someone to assist me. When I saw your ritual, I demonstrated respect and tried not to interrupt. I meant no harm or disrespect. Why are you doing this to me?

The color of our skin doesn't make us at war. That ended long ago."

"If you are done, I will continue," the old man's voice was steady and emotionless. Its tone indicated no sympathy would be rendered. "You witnessed a sacred ceremony. As a white man, you see no harm. Yet, your act is unacceptable to our gods, and to us. We are the religious leaders of our respective tribes. Although divided by distance, our faith is united. They brought you to us, not to kill, but to serve our purpose. Instead of one of our kind being taken and used by your people, you will take his place. You will become a living sacrifice—one that will live forever. Your punishment is that you will wish for your death each minute you survive. That is the gift our gods demand ... vengeance upon your kind ... vengeance against those that continue to steal our lands to this day, those who give promises and spread poverty and death in its place. The desires of our gods will be satisfied tonight."

The blades of those holding my legs sliced deep into my upper thighs, and into the cartilage and muscle surrounding the top of my femur. The nerves shot the pain through the top of my head, where it exploded, creating more stars to fill the sky above. The crunching and ripping noises of my legs being torn from my body filled my ears, between the screams shrieking from my throat, and the flames laid against the open wounds to seal in my precious body fluids, by searing the flesh black, created an agony I couldn't handle. I passed out.

When I woke, I discovered they'd continued and done the same to my arms. Attempting to squirm free, my efforts awakened the pain of the wounds and burns I'd endured. Writhing in agony, I screamed again and again, hoping my God would come to my rescue and end my suffering. Instead, a wooden cup was forced between my lips and a bitter liquid flowed into my mouth. I spat it out and was rewarded by several blows to the face. They tried again. I refused and received the same as before. Somewhat stunned, I gave up and swallowed the liquid.

Thick in nature, the concoction flowed slowly through my body. It burned as it traveled from my throat to my stomach. The pain intensified as it passed through my digestive organs and intestines, seeming to glue them shut. My ability to move any muscle departed. I lay still, like a wooden log, unable to show any semblance of life, but unable to stop my thoughts. I was wrapped in yellowed and moldy strips of hide, their odor that of rot and decay. A small slit remained open over my eyes, just enough for me to see through. It was a form of vengeance, an everlasting torture, to see life around me in which I could not participate.

"We have succeeded in making a mockery of your people," the old man's voice whispered, once we'd arrived at our destination. "They paid us to bring them one of our ancients ... one for them to make even more money from, for years to come. Instead, we bring them one of their own. Our people will not suffer the disgrace of being put on display. The honor of that disgrace will remain among those who fail to recognize the superior people. You pay the price for their vanity ... and will do so, forever."

I see the people walking in front of me ... white people ... tourists, flaunting expensive cameras and designer shoes. They gawk and make jokes, many discriminatory in nature—racist jokes about the "Indian mummy" as they pass by, teaching their children their tainted ways, passing on their disrespect from generation to generation, as they were taught by their ancestors.

I am in a new building, a museum—air conditioned, and lit with electric lights. Across the aisle are artifacts of a people thought to be long gone. Yet, I know the truth. They live today. They have pride and worship their gods, who are powerful, yet, very vengeful.

The irony of my serving punishment for the acts of my race is, instead of hating, I am loving. Yes, I love seeing all the new faces, and hearing different voices, day after day. I am still selling a product, one not as it seems, one portrayed as ancient ... of a race of which I am not. And, the best thing is, my customers are buying it. My life is a dream. I am a salesperson, and will always be a salesperson.

What could be better than that?

I Walk

The road beneath my feet echoes the sound of my heels pounding the pavement. Clouds creep between the moon and I, jealous of our relationship, making it difficult to see where the road travels. My right ankle aches, having been twisted and sent off course, as it had discovered the uneven edge of the pavement too often. Stopping would grant my pursuers permission to shorten the distance between us. It is permission I cannot give. Not if I am to kill again.

A break in the clouds provides a glimpse of a railroad crossing sign ahead. I gauge the distance, in case it is again hidden in the darkness—which comes only too soon. My westward trek becomes southerly, as my shuffling feet find the iron rails of the tracks and I turn off the road to follow them. I will be safer this way. No stray police officer will stop to question me here. I am sure the tracks will lead me to another town, somewhere down the line. A place where my innermost desires will once again be sated.

I slow my pace, not wanting to be tripped up by a broken railroad tie and face injury. My pursuers will follow the road, I'm sure, knowing I am a stranger to the area, and not one to veer from common routes. I have no doubts they know my identity. Word travels fast these days, and my journey has been filled with murder. There is no need to hide what I am. It is not my fault. Yet, finding anyone to believe those words would be impossible.

Two weeks ago, I was only a student at a small university. Like many young people, I'd found myself bored with traditional studies, and sought out others for mental stimulation. I ventured into the dark arts, Black Magic, witchcraft, if you will. Areas where mortal man had no right exploring, unless they wished to find a fate they'd not expected. Doors to unknown realms of evil had opened. Innocent, I'd played into their hands, and allowed myself to become a slave to their needs, their evil. I was helpless to ignore their orders, and became a tool for their enjoyment, something with which to toy.

And tonight I travel the way of the hobo.

I remember leaving the dorm that night, my head spinning, after having given up on getting any sleep. My body burned, as if a fire had been ignited deep within, and my muscles demanded I give them the exercise they required. I roamed between the streetlights, seeking to stay in the shadows, hidden from sight as a thief in the night. I cut between blocks, knowing the video cameras atop the intersection traffic signals would only catch a brief glimpse of me, blurred at best, in doing so. Behind the dense bushes accenting the multimillion-dollar buildings lining the street, I watched couple after couple walking back to their campus homes. None laughed or smiled. It was as if they'd been assigned a walking partner, not chosen one with which to share the evening.

My last date had been in high school. College had proven to be a waste for me, in that area. Too many girls believing there was a superior gender, and they were it. No need for men—satisfaction could be found with battery-driven devices and members of their own gender, while fantasizing of men becoming their slaves. I had always tried to treat women with respect, but these bitches were looking for a reason to claim you violated their rights, and get you kicked out of school for sexual abuse. I didn't need them, not with the game playing they insisted upon. My hand worked just fine, and didn't need batteries.

Around the corner of the building came the aroma of burning marijuana. I crept to the edge and knelt, peering around the brick with the greatest of care. I recognized the uniform of a campus security guard, armed only with a walkie talkie, facing down the street, away from me. Hired to keep the building safe from vandals at night, this rent-a-cop was out smoking a joint, and getting paid for it. As a car drove by, its lights showed he was wearing earphones, probably connected to his phone. Not only was he getting high, he was listening to music while doing so.

Normally, this would not have bothered me. In fact, I probably would have asked him for a hit. But, from deep inside, an anger rose. Unlike any I'd ever experienced, my ire continued to grow, until I stood and charged the guard from behind. I hit him full-force with all my weight, and drove him face-first into the thick bushes.

He struggled to free himself and reached for his walkie talkie, not realizing it was now in my hand. I thrust the sole of my shoe into his back repeatedly, finally feeling the spine crunch under its weight. I rolled him over and stared into his eyes, reflecting pain and fear. Again, using my feet as killing weapons, I squelched his screams with a foot to the throat, not yielding any mercy until his eyes stopped blinking.

I would have no more worry of his screams being heard.

A rush of elation flowed through my body. I was never a fighter, nor a bully, instead, I'd always been the victim. Seeing the results of my attack, I stifled a need to rear my head back and release a loud, maniacal laugh—one of satisfaction and joy—as this rent-a-cop would never again act out his fantasies of superiority upon the innocent, as many of his kind are known to do. Justice had been served, and he lay dead. I glowed with pride as I trod away from the scene, in the shadows.

Back in my dorm room, the aggression that had taken me over departed, and a feeling of guilt hit. Disbelief at my actions clawed away at my sanity, and I cringed at the thought of having taken a life. A fear of being caught took hold, and a life behind bars became an inevitable possibility. I knew I could never lie my way out of a police investigation—my feelings of guilt would betray me. I battled between turning myself in, and fleeing, knowing neither an attractive option. In my head, laughter roared, the laughter of another, the laughter of the one who had taken over my mind and made me do the dastardly deed. A reality smacked me across the face and returned to slam me in the gut—I was possessed.

I decided upon a third option, to deny the event had taken place, and continue my life as I would normally do. I tried attending classes over the next few days, but the paranoia of being caught wouldn't leave. My studies mattered not, as I was constantly looking over my shoulder for those seeking the murderer and wanting to protect the other innocents on the university campus. I dreaded the possibility of my being controlled once more, and another dying to amuse the one I housed deep inside—the one who could make his appearance whenever he chose—leaving me to suffer the consequences.

It was time to leave campus. Yeah, I've left all right. I've left, and now I'm walking on a railroad track, in the middle of nowhere.

Packing a few things in my backpack, I took one of the city's loaner bikes to the "Thank You for Visiting ..." sign and dropped it there. It was too recognizable to ride any farther. A teenager pulled over and gave me a lift after only a few minutes of my thumb begging for a ride. He was a nice kid who'd been checking out the university, to see if it would be a place he'd like to attend after high school. Almost immediately, we stopped for gas down the road, where it was cheaper than in the city. I couldn't blame the kid. I was well familiar with trying to save to afford college. After we traveled a few miles, I apologized for not going at the station, but asked him to pull over so I could take a leak. Trouble was, it wasn't me asking. He waited patiently and took a swig from a bottle he'd grabbed from under his seat. He never saw me pull the jack knife from my pocket. Never saw me shove it in his chest, either. Even with his eyes permanently open, he never saw me pull his body from the car and drop it down into the ditch, off the road. I couldn't take his money, though. Figured he might have a younger brother or sister who could use it for their college fund.

It was getting easier for the demon within to take control. I guess a little practice never hurts.

The next day, I disposed of the car in a grocery store parking lot. I couldn't take a chance on his parents notifying the police of his disappearance, and getting caught with it. I'd searched the glove compartment and found a small caliber pistol the kid must have been keeping for protection. Too bad he was the trusting type. He could've used it. My plans were to keep walking, and stay away from people as much as possible. My conscience was beginning to bother me about the two deaths, and there was no need to add to the guilt. Those were my thoughts. The demon had others.

Passing by a department store, I witnessed a man lifting a child up by one arm and using his other to whip the child's bottom. To add insult to injury, the man scolded the child (at the top of his lungs) to control himself better in public. The hypocrisy of his actions set off my internal anger, once more. As he shoved the child into the backseat and slammed the door, I hurried to get to him before he was able to close his. After one pistol shot to the head, he would no longer be beating another child ... ever again. Yanking his body out of the driver's seat, I took his place and drove off, aware the child behind me was scared to death. The voice inside my head said, "Don't leave him scarred for life. End his suffering." I pulled into an alley and pulled the trigger, putting a bullet between the boy's eyes to end his suffering.

Leaving the car behind, I resumed my efforts to get out of town. Glancing at myself in a store window, I was surprised to see my face dotted with red spots, probably blood from shooting the youngster at such close range. I walked into a convenience store and straight to their restroom. Washing off the blood took a few minutes. I took off my shirt, which also had a few spatters of blood around the shoulders, and grabbed a spare from my backpack. Selecting a couple of bottles of water from their cooler, I headed toward the counter.

A heated argument was in process about the amount of change that had been given back to the customer. The loud debate over the amount given for payment continued for several minutes, with the clerk finally telling the customer to see the manager in the morning. When the customer had balked, the clerk reached under the counter, pulled out a pistol, and repeated his directions. The customer took his suggestion, cussing all the way out.

Standing just around the aisle, I watched the grinning clerk open the cash drawer, pocketing a ten-dollar-bill. I walked up, set the bottles on the counter, and shot the clerk in the face—killing him instantly. Taking the bill from his pocket, I set it under the drawer of the register, grabbed the pistol he'd brandished, and left a couple of dollars for my water, before exiting. I had no doubt the entire episode had been caught on the store's video system, but the voice inside demanded I continue down the highway.

Now, I'm on a railroad track. The sun is rising to my left, making it easier to see where my steps are headed. I no longer fear tripping and injuring myself. My pace quickens.

There is a small house ahead. As I near, an old dog rises and comes my direction. It nears, and I see the dog is not just skinny, it is barely anything but bones. I look over to the field adjoining the home and watch an old cow, in a similar state, leaning heavily against a barn, too weak to stand without support. From the home, the smell of bacon cooking fills the air and my stomach growls. I'm sure the stomachs of the animals I've seen are long past that stage.

I go into stealth mode and approach the house, stealing glances into the windows I pass. I only see an old man, standing at the stove as his breakfast cooks. He is unkempt, dirty, as if he no longer cares about his hygiene. His closeness to death has eliminated his caring about the life of his animals. He obviously feels they should suffer, as he is doing. Yet, he is doing so with a full stomach.

The voice inside of me screams out. My arm raises, and I empty the remaining shells of the teenager's pistol into the man, through the window. His head shows the entrance points of two of the bullets and he falls to his side, tumbling over a kitchen chair and onto his dirty floor. He will suffer no more.

I kick in his old back door and enter. I search the home for anyone I might have missed in my search. There are none. He had been alone. I go to the stove, remove the bacon and eggs from the pan, and take them outside to the dog. They vanish in seconds and his tail wags—I'm sure for the first time in years. I go to the barn and find a little grain remaining in a burlap bag. I pour it into a trough and watch as the cow's shaky legs barely support her weight, as she walks to it and begins to feed. I hope someone will find the animals and save them from their suffering. They deserve better.

After preparing a second breakfast and eating, I make a few sandwiches from the lunchmeat I find in the fridge, and toss the remaining slices to the dog. His tail wags again, in thanks. Before leaving, I set fire to the curtains in the bedroom, hoping they'll gradually set the house ablaze. It should help to draw attention to the plight of the animals.

I have difficulty understanding my demon. It has no respect for human life, but cannot tolerate wrong doing or suffering. I have been commanded to kill, time and time again, experiencing less remorse with each instance of violence. I am a killer, and will continue to kill, until stopped. The demon will not leave me. It will laugh at death and rile itself at those who do not follow the path of righteousness. It is the devil's voice of hypocrisy, let loose upon the weaknesses of humans. It will never stop on its own.

The road beneath my feet again echoes the sound of my heels pounding the pavement. Clouds creep between the moon and I, jealous of our relationship, making it difficult to see where the road travels. My right ankle still aches, having been twisted and sent off course as it had discovered the uneven edge of the pavement too often. Stopping would grant my pursuers permission to shorten the distance between us. It is permission I cannot give.

Not if I am to kill again.

Starting Over

Ten years have passed since the world was turned upside down. It seems longer.

I miss seeing the sun in the sky. The haze we live in acts to filter our view, and its warmth. Four layers of clothing barely allow us to survive in the cold surrounding us. One has to find shelter for the darkness hours, as the temperatures will freeze exposed skin without mercy, and the violent winds will rip it apart. We huddle together in fear as the lightning storms drop more and more snow, knowing it will never melt. All single-story structures have vanished underneath, and provide dangerous holes and gullies, where roofs have caved in under its weight.

We are lucky to find a place to protect us from the elements, as walls have grown weak from the constant pelting they receive. We work to strengthen and protect our shelters with various materials we find—wooden sheets of plywood or metal, and even tarps in emergencies—but we have to be on the constant lookout for new homes, in case they collapse.

Starvation is another threat to our existence. We use old maps and city directories to locate old grocery stores, but find more in the emptiness of the deserted mansions. Our small group depends on me to keep them alive. I do my best. Yet, there are days we spend hours digging in the snow to find an entrance to a building, only to find it previously raided by those before us. It is not the life we want, but it is the life we have been forced to live.

Most of the wealthy population had been taken to survival centers, as they were deemed necessary to survive and lead the world recovery, when possible. Miscalculations in supply needs, and the demands the wealthy would make, quickly turned those locations into prison camps. Suicide became a daily occurrence, as did rioting. It was expected by us commoners. The wealthy had never experienced the need to be tolerant of being ordered around, nor conservative in luxury demands. Their minds were unable to cope with the struggles most of our current survivors had to incur, before the disaster happened.

Yes, we had warnings. For two years, we were told the asteroid would hit and destroy the Earth. Its size was such, the experts saw no chance of man surviving. Of course, our governments feared that the news would create chaos in the streets, so they minimized the danger. What the experts stated as one-third the size of the Earth, the government stated the asteroid was only as big as a small apartment building. If it hit at all, its damage would be hardly noticed. Propaganda ran rampant as newspapers and television spread their lies, older movies depicting ways to destroy the asteroid were utilized to calm our fears, and keep us living our lives as normally as possible. Still, there was a feeling in the air many experienced—a premonition of impending disaster. Retirement savings were withdrawn, and the banks suffered, some closing as their funds grew thin. Violence increased and shots were heard constantly, as the threats of extended prison sentences were laughed at.

The six months before impact were progressively worse. Photos of the asteroid, and information about its true size, were leaked to the public. Estimations of death of the Earth's population soared to ninety percent or more, some stating man would become extinct within hours. Survivalists stocked up on all the food they could gather, grocery store deliveries were hijacked, and semi-trailers filled with supplies hidden in barns and other buildings. Grocery stores hired armed guards to protect what they had on their shelves. No one wanted to believe they would die immediately upon impact. All had a plan.

Most died before they could use it.

We are lucky at times, and find one of the trailers filled with supplies. We know enough to conserve and not waste them, as they may never be replaced. A full trailer can last us a year or two, depending upon what it holds. We have little use for mops and home cleaning supplies, but the food items are beneficial. Dates on cans are ignored, as the cans and packages have been frozen solid since only weeks after the asteroid hit. We'll take a chance on food poisoning. It's better than starving.

So is cannibalism.

Yes, we consume the dead. We are beyond the social mores and religious convictions—we have to do what we must to live. We still find frozen victims in the snow—the cold keeping them from decomposing—that meant meat for the dinner table. We joke about how human flesh tastes like chicken, as if any of us remember how fresh chicken tasted. It is protein we need to survive, yet seeing it being cooked over an open fire brings a queasiness to one's stomach.

Occasionally, we will see other survivors seeking food, as well. We will always act friendly, until we scope out how many the others have in their groups, and where they're located. If they are alone, they become our dinner. If they are a member of a group, we will meet with them, sometimes offering them a chance to feast. We simply forego telling them they will be the main course. The look on their faces when they discover that fact is a moment to remember.

We are hoping for one of those moments today.

Yesterday, one of our search parties located another group. They found it consisted of many women, something ours does not. The thought of female companionship after all these years is tempting—too tempting to ignore. It is our plan to kill the males and make the females ours. Those who refuse, will join their previous companions on our dinner table. Those who accept, will live.

As they arrive, we see the women are younger, probably just children when the asteroid hit our planet. They are very slender, probably like us, from lack of food, but still hold promise to satisfy needs not attended to in almost a decade. We are the perfect hosts, sharing more than we should, and making them comfortable with our group. They suspect nothing when our males rise, being told to get the special gifts we've prepared for them. Weapons in hand, death is fast as throats are cut and hearts punctured. The women are told to assist in taking the bodies outside, to be buried in the snow. There they will freeze and be preserved for later meals. To our surprise, there is no resistance, and very few tears. These will be worthy additions to our group— strong and intelligent enough to understand one does what it takes to survive.

We find they had just joined the murdered males a few days before. No relationships had been made, as they'd been told to take their time and choose their mates when ready. We will not give them that opportunity. Our members choose, and take their new companions behind the tarps serving as room dividers. There, they pleasure themselves until exhausted. It has been too long since stomachs have been full, and sex enjoyed. Sleep comes easily.

I am alone, having chosen none. It had been my practice to ignore women, or any relationship, as it would only serve as an emotional distraction to my leadership. I awoke seconds ago to the sound of screams. Before I could rise, my curtain opened and one of the women stood before me holding a bloody knife.

"We thank you for the meal you provided, and for the meat you will provide in the future. If you hadn't have invited us here tonight, it was in our plans to do as you did, to our own males. We appreciate you doing the work for us. Your group will be greatly appreciated in the future."

Another joined her, also holding a bloody knife, and together they advanced. Yes, they were indeed intelligent, and willing to do what needed to be done to survive.

I hope they choke on me.

Let's Tour the Graveyard

"C'mon down. It only narrows up for a few feet, and then it opens wide again."

Echoing deep from the bend in the passage, came the voice of my friend. I was reluctant, but after months of asking me to join him spelunking, I had agreed. Now, I was fighting the darkness, and my swelling fear inside.

I should have continued to say, "No."

Being older, I had foolishly ignored my experience in a similar environment, during my youth. My parents had taken me to Mammoth Cave, in Kentucky. During a tour, the guide had switched off all lighting to demonstrate the total darkness of the cave system. I had panicked. The tightening in my chest restricted my lungs from expanding. The need for air became apparent, and I reached out for my mother to help. Yet, in the pitch black, couldn't find her. I dropped to my knees and fell forward, the palms of my hands finding the cool damp stone of the cave floor. Scrambling to find my mother, I cried out. The lights came on and the embarrassment of being the center of everyone's stares filled my body, making me wish for the darkness to return and provide me a place to hide.

Yet, here I was, once again, alone with the darkness surrounding me, except for a small beam of light coming from the light on my hard hat. It was the only thing in existence keeping my panic from running wild, as if the shrinking passage, which threatened to hold me captive for eternity, wasn't bad enough.

We had reached a point where my friend's smaller size was a major advantage. He had slid through the narrowing gaps, with ease. My larger build had hindered me being able to do the same, and allowed the sharp rocks to snag and rip my t-shirt and tender torso in several places. My six-foot frame was squished in a three-by-two-foot tunnel, even in a prone position. Fighting to follow my friend, I scooted forward an inch at a time, against a passage growing smaller as I progressed.

"C'mon, you can do it," he shouted out from ahead, oblivious to my plight. "It gets wider once you get through the next bend."

I turned on my side and continued, my shoulders crammed against the floor and ceiling. My arms stretched out in front of me, I grasped for handholds to assist my forward movement. The pressure of the rock against my back and stomach became greater, tightening until inhaling air became difficult. I could see the bend, only a few feet away. Reaching out, my fingers gripped the last bit of outcropping, and I used every muscle in my arms to pull forward.

A tremendous weight squeezed my body as I stopped, only a foot from the bend. No matter how hard I struggled, I couldn't move forward. I was stuck. Battling a panic attack, I pushed against the rocks, attempting to slide back, to where my chest could expand enough to breathe. No good. I couldn't move.

"I can't move!" I screamed, not knowing how my friend could help. He couldn't make me shrink in size, and with the bend between us, his strength to pull me forward would be negligible. "Are you there? I said I can't move!"

Had he moved on without me? There was no response, of any type. Here I was, stuck in a tunnel, and no one to help me through. Surely, there would be another exit ahead. Maybe, just maybe, he'd seen my situation coming and had went on to get help. Then again, what if there wasn't another exit? What if I was blocking his way out?

I screamed for him to answer, over and over. Nothing but silence. I threw my head back to scream again, smashing my hard hat against the rock wall. The lens of my head lamp shattered, and darkness enveloped me. I was trapped. I would die here. No one would come to my rescue. I wiggled and struggled to escape, screaming to God for mercy—for some miracle to occur and take me from this living grave.

"Charles, wake up, Charles! You're having a nightmare. For God's sake, wake up!"

Darkness was replaced with a blinding light. I raised my hands to shield my eyes from the orb, and found the bulb of my bedside lamp the culprit. Christine shook me, hoping to bring me back to reality, and escape the nightmare that had been so real, so lifelike.

"I'm okay," I whispered, hoping to believe my own words. "It was only a dream. I'm awake now."

"You better be," she whispered, her words bordering upon a threatening tone, "I didn't imagine that this would be the way we spent our first night together as husband and wife. Don't you dare fall asleep on the plane. I'd hate to have to explain this to the attendants."

"I just need some water. I'll be back."

Starting to the bathroom, I changed my mind and headed to the kitchen. Space ... I needed space to get myself together. Letting the water run to get cold, I quickly lost patience and grabbed a couple of ice cubes from the freezer. Shaking the glass for maximum effect, I took a long drink. The liquid numbed my throat and caused a quick shiver, as it reached my stomach. Standing over the sink, I drained the glass over my head. I was refreshed—alive once more—as the icy liquid drained off my chin. Wiping dry with a dish towel, I sat at the table and took a moment to analyze what had taken place.

So many possibilities to consider. A premonition, or a result of all that had transpired? Had a hidden fear of the commitments and responsibilities of marriage surfaced in my subconscious? Could the images, still so crystal clear in my mind, of being trapped and crushed in darkness, be fears of being caught in a place I didn't belong for the rest of my life? Or, could the nightmare have a deeper meaning? Did something lay ahead, like a menacing lion, waiting to pounce when I least expected it. Whatever it was, I had to put the nightmare behind me and get to bed. Tomorrow was a big day—one of travel and a new beginning. Our first night had been a disaster, thanks to the nightmare. Another mess up couldn't be allowed to occur.

In the morning, our honeymoon to South America became a reality. We had purchased tickets well in advance to save money, as well as scheduled the cheapest of transportation. No direct flights for us— strictly puddle jumpers. Three stops between Atlanta and Dallas, before our main flight to Panama. It would take longer, but would save us substantially.

Leaving the plane in Panama City, the heat and humidity smacked us in the face. We'd departed Atlanta in the middle of a heat wave, but Panama's close proximity to the Equator made Atlanta's temperature seem cool. Both Christine and I broke into an immediate sweat, it didn't seep from every pore, it flowed, in streams. It didn't take long for our clothes to be drenched, or for Christine to start complaining about its effect on her hair. It was almost as bad inside the airport, with its ineffective air conditioning system. Only the absence of the sun's rays made it somewhat tolerable.

Our bus to the next step of our journey, Bogota, Colombia, didn't leave until early the next morning. Our room at one of the city's premier hotels proved to have air conditioning as effective as the airport's. Figuring a sauna was the last thing we needed, we set out to find a cooler place, away from the afternoon heat. After a few blocks of searching, we found a small bar that fit the bill. Feeling human again, we filled the next couple of hours with drinks, a small dinner, and small talk about our future together, and the lies we'd have to tell our friends once we got back home, about having a great time.

With the sun setting, we decided to take a chance on the air conditioning being fixed, and returned to our hotel. It wasn't. In fact, we opened a window to the room and found the outside air temperature a bit cooler. Our second night of being man and wife proved to be a sweaty affair—not just because of the torrid bedroom action, but the humidity drained our bodies of the salty fluid. Christine soon tired of the sweat dripping from my chin onto her face and put an end to the event, before either of us were satisfied. Frustrated, sleep didn't come easy to either of us.

Waking before sunrise, we envisioned lovemaking in a cool shower would make things right. Imagine our disappointment when we discovered even the cold water coming from the showerhead was too warm to enjoy ourselves. Tempers to a boiling point, we dressed and made a hasty exit from the hotel.

There seemed to be no escape from the heat. By the time we had walked to the bus station, our clothes were dripping with sweat. We had arrived early, hoping to sit back in air conditioning, with a cup of coffee. Finding the windows open, and no vending machine in operational order, we positioned ourselves under the single ceiling fan in the place, and prayed for the bus to be air-conditioned.

The few locals in the place eyed us with suspicion. It was my guess they imagined us spending the night in the station, seeing how we appeared. Across the way, one refused to stop staring our direction. Ignoring my telling her she was presentable, Christine headed off to the ladies' room to check herself out. I thought his eyes would follow her shapely body there, but they remained on me. Having read warnings of the constant threat of robberies in the area, I glanced around the waiting area for something I could use as a weapon, if necessary. Besides a metal rack screwed to the wall, containing a few travel brochures, nothing was nearby that would serve as a weapon. Christine's return provided me with a plastic hair brush. If needed, I could jab him with the handle. It wasn't much, but it would have to do.

The minutes passed at a snail's pace. My nerves created attack scenes in my mind, and ways I might be able to defend us. I whispered various directions to my wife, should he come close, and pointed out the nearest exits where she could run for help.

"If you keep thinking like this, I'm going to get paranoid," she replied with a nervous giggle. "Besides, if we were going to be robbed, I don't think anyone would do it while sitting in a bus station."

"That's what they expect you to think," I whispered back. "They like to catch you when you think you're safe."

A long, silver bus pulled up in front of the station, brakes squealing as it came to a stop. Our would-be robber stood, straightened his pants, and headed out to meet it. I watched as he opened the luggage door on the side of the vehicle and began unloading the baggage for the passengers debarking. He returned to the door and announced the bus was loading up all passengers to Bogota. Obviously, my fears had been unfounded. I handed him our bags to load, fumbling with the hairbrush still in my hand, and gave him a good-sized tip for doing so. Slightly embarrassed, I almost made it to the door before Christine asked, "If you think we won't be attacked now, could I have my hairbrush back?"

The bus ride to Bogota was fantastic. The air conditioning was better than any we'd experienced since leaving the plane, even that of the restaurant. We'd laughed about my worries of being robbed a couple of times—Christine not being the type to let it die—but I was still concerned. The man who had loaded our bags, was also a passenger on the bus. On a quick visit to the tiny onboard restroom, I'd nodded to him, thinking the tip would create a bond of sorts. Yet, his response had been the same icy stare we'd been given in the station. After returning to my seat, I debated on telling her about what I'd seen. I knew she'd say I was being paranoid— which was probably the truth. I decided silence was the answer.

We arrived in Bogota without incident, and found the hotel to be much like those we had left behind in the states. Great air conditioning, hot and cold running water, and a good overall cleanliness was present. It was almost a shame to dirty up the sheets, making up for lost time in Panama City. Lying together naked, all we'd been through was put in the past, and only our future mattered. Married and betrothed to one another forever, we could enjoy the good times, and persevere through the bad. That was what marriage was supposed to be like, according to those who had preached to us prior to our wedding day.

Only having eaten a couple of pieces of fruit since the night before, our growling stomachs reminded us it was time to take care of them. We showered, dressed, and took to the streets, to see what the city offered. Finding a small café, we were instantly greeted by a waiter and asked if we had been there before. Stating we hadn't, as we'd just been married, he turned and announced our newlywed status to all the patrons. Cheers and applause filled the place and our backsides were patted by many, as we made our way to our table. Immediately, two drinks were set in front of us, courtesy of one of the patrons. The chef left his kitchen to tell us anything on the menu was free, and to order whatever we wished. More drinks arrived, one after the other, as we dined, as well as the good wishes of many making toasts in our honor.

I'd drank way too many drinks, but found it hard to refuse when another set were placed on the table. Raising my glass, I noticed our companion from the station and bus, sitting in the back of the room. I finished my drink and glanced back to where he'd been seated, only to find an empty table and chair.

We awoke in our hotel room the next morning, both suffering terrible hangovers. Neither of us wanted to talk to the other, as listening was too painful. Only after a few aspirin, and a cup of coffee, did we discover neither remembered returning to the hotel the night before. In fact, all we recalled were the multiple toasts and endless glasses of alcohol we consumed. Grateful to be safe and sound, our late awakening had created another problem. We had missed the bus to Machala, Ecuador. Calling the hotel desk, we were informed there was another bus scheduled for departure there, the next morning. Like it or not, we were going to spend another night where we were at.

We spent most of the day recuperating from our night of drinking. Not quite by accident, we found making love was a great way to sweat out the alcohol, and kill some time. It was so good that we decided once was not enough. Much later, we passed out from sheer exhaustion.

We woke well after dark, famished. Deciding on a return visit to the club we'd had such a great time at the night before, we retraced our steps, in hopes of a great meal and promises of much less to drink. It wasn't very late, but the streets were empty in comparison to the previous evening. Besides an occasional beggar asking for a handout, we were the only ones out and about.

Finally, we arrived at our destination—or so we thought. The club, which had been filled to capacity last night, was abandoned. The entrance had been blocked, and sheets of plywood had been nailed over the windows. It was difficult for us to believe this had been the scene of such a joyous evening, only hours before. As we returned to the hotel, I saw a familiar figure skirting into an alley ahead. Our shadow was still with us.

We left town the next morning and headed to Machala. Although a much older bus than the first, the seats were comfortable, and its air conditioning kept us cool. The landscape had changed from city and suburbia, to a dense and wild jungle. Its beauty was a temptation to explore, but knowledge of the perils within made it foolish to consider. There were many dangers here—unlike those we dealt with in Atlanta. Hand in hand, we sat, grateful for the safety the bus provided.

This leg of our trip would take two days. Glimpses of tropical birds, and the dead bodies of unfamiliar roadkill, quickly became our only excitement. The obligatory crying baby plagued us from time to time, as did the snoring of an elderly couple sitting behind us. Our old acquaintance was still accompanying us, again riding alone, in the back of the bus. His ominous presence did nothing to ease our restroom visits, but his actions did nothing to endanger our wellbeing. If he had been friendly in the least, I might have asked him about the boarding up of the club we'd all been at, or why he had missed yesterday's bus, as we had.

The jostling and bouncing of the ride took its toll on our bodies. Pulling into a small town, around dusk, we discovered this was to be our sleepover location. We debarked and took a moment to stretch our legs and enjoy the scenery. The fresh air, though warm, was filled with scents of the surrounding jungle. Some beautiful flowers caught Christine's eye and she ventured over for a closer look. A shadow blurred by me and charged in her direction. The glint of a raised machete, swinging downward, caused me to scream out Christine's name in warning and start forward. She turned and fell back at the sight of the oncoming blade. Barely missing her, the machete's edge sliced down like a lightning bolt, and sliced the head off a venomous Eyelash Viper, only inches away from where her hand had been.

The man picked up the bottom half of the snake's body and used it to maneuver the top portion onto the wide blade. For a moment, he toyed with it, watching the snake bite at the bottom time and time again. Taking them off to the side, he picked up an old portion of a broken cement building block and slammed it down, crushing the deadly viper's head. Its fangs would strike no more. A devious smile crossed his face as he examined his handy work. Almost regrettably, he gathered the two sections of the snake and tossed them into the underbrush. Without so much as a glance, he walked back toward the bus.

Christine's near-death experience didn't alarm her as much as it had me. I had been city born and bred, while she had been raised in the swamp lands, outside of the metro area. While I was a bundle of nerves and felt the need to hold and comfort her, Christine pushed me away and scolded herself for not seeing the snake. "I've got to be more aware. That was damn stupid of me. If it had been a Cottonmouth, it would have tagged me good."

Our overnight stay in the small town was without air conditioning. A large, squeaking ceiling fan provided a little cooling, but neither of us got much sleep. Our dinner had consisted of a tasty soup, but the spices provided for an evening of trips to the toilet, as our bodies refused to process it. I searched for our "friend", both during dinner and at breakfast, but had no luck. He had disappeared, without me being able to thank him for saving Christine's life. His absence was noted as we boarded the bus and continued down the road. For the first time, I found myself wishing he was still with us.

The remainder of the journey to Machala was uneventful. We arrived late that evening, purchased some native fruit from a vendor, and headed to our hotel—exhausted. We found the lack of air-conditioned rooms made for uninvited guests, who found their way in through the open windows, mosquitoes. The pesky critters discovered a way to join us under the netting as we slept, and we woke the next morning with multiple bites. As we dabbed alcohol on the bites, we wondered out loud about how much blood we'd lost to the blood suckers, and when the malaria would set in.

Doesn't sound like much of a honeymoon destination, does it?

Part of the money for our trip had been received from a grant Christine had been able to procure from the university. She was one of their top sociologists, and been able to persuade the department head to fund the studies she could make of a nearby ghost town, setting just outside of La Noria. There, rumors of supernatural rituals bred interest in the eyes of her upper-level professors. As details of these had been virtually impossible to acquire, Christine's findings would hopefully bring both her, and the university, some valuable respect.

So, the last leg of our trip began with another bus ride. This one would last three days. Neither of us looked forward to it, but there were no other options. Thanks to missing the bus in Bogota, we couldn't chance another delay. Time was running out.

We arrived in La Noria feeling as if we'd been tortured. We had—the bouncing about on the terrible roads, no overnight stops, and poor offering of food stops provided it. Our destination hotel offered none of the comforts we needed. Pathetic housekeeping, and no air conditioning, made the room a nest for every kind of insect making its home in the area. Hoping to find something edible, we indulged ourselves in some of the food being cooked over open fires along the streets, afraid to ask what we were eating. Fighting the constant humming of the mosquito swarms, we had a couple of beers and returned to the hotel for another night of feeding the local insect population while we slept.

A new day did nothing to improve upon my attitude. Neither did the lukewarm water leaving the showerhead, in a murky brown color. I sat, frustrated, knowing that Christine's naked body was immersed in it as I watched the various types of cockroaches and beetles scurry around the floor and walls. Our decision to keep our bags zipped tight, and not unpack, had been a wise one. At least none of these invaders would hitchhike home with us. Atlanta needed no other types of bugs. It had plenty of its own.

Christine's mood was disgusting. It was my first time to a third world country, she had visited them on several occasions and was somewhat accustomed to the inconveniences. To her, any shower water was better than bathing in a river, and bugs were a part of life. As I stomped around, attempting to annihilate the intruders, her giggles and laughter soon infected my psyche. I had found humor in my misery, thanks to her. It was to be the best part of my day.

Christine's excitement about getting to the ghost town was contagious, as well. We located a driver to take us, first to Plura to grab a bite to eat, and then onward, to the site. He was a friendly gent, but very much the quiet type. He answered most questions with a "Yes" or "No" and added no more. We couldn't complain about his driving, though. He missed most of the deep ruts, and maneuvered the vehicle as if he'd been born doing so.

The ghost town was nothing like I'd expected. Too many old Western movies had given me the idea this would be a place where gangs of outlaws resided in deserted saloons, while tumbleweeds blew down dusty streets. How wrong I had been. Here, modern buildings of brick and stone lined the cobblestone streets. We could have been in any of the other towns we'd passed through in the last few days. Only the people were missing. There were, however, plenty of vendors, awaiting the tours to come before the day's end. Their numbers grew as we approached the graveyard, as if they knew it to be the center of activity.

A shiver passed through me. Activity and graveyard were two words normally not associated together.

Massive tombstones lined the rows ahead of us. Some displayed the effects of time and weather, while others appeared to be new. None were of any special design or detail. Still, Christine rushed around, taking her notes and pictures, with the enthusiasm of a Black Friday shopper. This was her territory, her specialty. To me, it was just another place where dead people were buried—nothing more, nothing less.

The heat of the afternoon began to get to me. Not wanting to be a bother to Christine, I took shelter in the shade of a small chapel, in the center of the graveyard. Checking the grass for ants and snakes, I decided it was as good a place as any to spend the afternoon. Sitting back against the mortar, I dozed off.

I must have been wearier than I'd thought, as the sunset filled the sky upon my awakening. I was surprised to see the evening had vastly increased the number in attendance, tenfold—more and more arriving in groups each minute. Some were chanting as they gathered, in a language that mixed derivatives of Portuguese and Spanish with something else. Its meaning was beyond my understanding.

I spotted Christine at the far end of the masses. Doing her job, she was still taking pictures and notes of all she was observing. I hurried to join her. "This is interesting, but are you sure we're not in any danger?"

"You are a Fraidy Cat, aren't you?" Her smile told me she wasn't as sure about our safety as she wanted me to believe. "Tell you what, let's step out of the group and take some pictures from a distance. It might be more interesting to observe the full ceremony from a distance, anyway."

There was resistance to our departing the main body. Several members of the group made feeble attempts to block our exiting, even snagging Christine's camera bag at times. The volume of the chanting increased, and most displayed the look of being under a hypnotic spell. Finally, we were able to force our way through a group of smaller women and take refuge outside the masses, on the side of a small hill, behind some bushes.

I was ready to leave, but had no idea if our driver was waiting, or a member of the group before us. The trip back was well beyond walking distance, and filled with unknown dangers. At least here, we knew what we were facing. Besides, Christine wouldn't even consider leaving. She was too busy documenting the event with pictures and notes.

The intensity of the chanting grew into a deafening roar. Their numbers had grown such that they now were able to encircle the entire graveyard, and began to fill up the interior grounds. I found myself beginning to hum the tune of the chant, not knowing the words. Shaking my head, I fought to clear it and regain my sanity.

"It looks like they're digging up two of the newer graves," she whispered as she adjusted her telephoto lens to focus on a section where workers were shoveling furiously. "Why would they ever do that? There's no sense to it."

"Let's go … now!" Grabbing her arm, I yanked her up and pulled her with me. She gave objections, but I was beyond listening. We were not invited here, and could be in real danger. If her job blinded her to that, it was my job to make her see. Finally giving in, she followed me to the parking lot. There, just ahead, sat the jeep in which we'd arrived. Frantic to find the keys, I searched under the seats and up under the dash. Nothing.

"Are you looking for these?"

I turned to see our old acquaintance, dangling the keys to the jeep from his fingers.

"I had to make sure you and your wife would get here safe. You have no idea how important you are to tonight's festivities. You might say you two are the featured guests. All have gathered here to see how well you perform."

Christine's scream rang out from behind me. I spun around to see one of the women we'd pushed our way through swing a shovel and clang it against her head. Reaching for her dropping body, another shovel found the back of my own, sending me into a world of sharp pain and darkness.

I came to gazing up into the face of the man who had followed us throughout our journey. His words were only garbles, at first, but cleared up as the fog in my mind departed. Although heavy in local accent, I gradually began to understand.

"As I was saying, I must give thanks to you and your beautiful wife, for enduring the hardships of the journey from your home to ours. As I know you're wondering what is to take place, please give me a moment to explain. My brother and his wife were on their honeymoon and killed in a mudslide, a few months ago. They were buried here, in sacred ground, until a couple matching them in marriage and love could be found as their replacements. Soon, they will be up and among the living, once more, as you assume their place among the dead. I wish you had someone to do the same for you, and could return to us, but I know that is not the case. I wish you well in the next life. Until then, enjoy your resting place."

No, this couldn't be happening! I tried to rise, but my arms and legs were bound. The scooting of the wooden lid, and the hammering of nails, told me it was true—we were to be buried alive! The coffin was lifted, and I could feel the swaying of the lines holding it, as it dropped deep within the hole that was to be my grave. I could do nothing as the sounds of the dirt being shoveled atop it went from loud to minor thuds. There was no escape.

I'm sure Christine lies in the grave next to me. Perhaps she knows what has taken place. If not, her sanity upon awakening will be put to the ultimate test. She will find herself trapped in the darkness, as I did in my dream. She will be unable to move in any direction, and her screams will not be answered. Madness will set in long before her air runs out.

I wish I could wake her, as she did me. Yet, it is not possible. I am going to lie here and die, peacefully, while enjoying the cool, dampness of being underground.

Right now, it's better than air conditioning.

Night Strolling

Ain't like the old days ... back when walking was about the only way you got somewhere. Oh, we had bicycles back then, but most of the roads weren't good enough to ride them on. Most of them had those big "balloon" type tires, three times the size you find anymore. They helped cushion the bumps, so the seat didn't wind up permanently inserted in your ass. These tiny little tires on bikes these days wouldn't last ten minutes back then. Oh, I know you got them fancy bikes you ride off mountains and shit, but I ain't talkin' about them. I'm talkin' the normal bikes ... the ones these idiots who put on skintight clothes and act like they're special by riding in the middle of the road on. Damned fools ... if they knew how many times I almost hit them on purpose, they'd change their ways.

I love to walk, especially at night. No, I'm not one of the dumbasses who walk in the road, when there are sidewalks made for them to walk on. Kind of like those joggers who do the same thing. Fools ... streets are for vehicles and sidewalks are for people. If you haven't figured that out yet, you're dumber than you'll look after I run over your ass.

No, like I said, I'm a night walker, a stroller, if you will. There's something about the cool night air that's refreshing—makes me feel alive. My old bones don't get much exercise. Yeah, I tried doing the "old people walking around the mall" thing. Wasn't much fun. Felt like I was shuffling along with a bunch of people doing a death march. Teenagers were a pain in the ass, too. They kept yelling out insults and weaving in and out, trying to trip up their elders. Little bastards, if they'd have tried it on me, I'd have sliced their balls off.

At times, you can find me in residential areas, around all the rich folks and their illuminated castles. Those folks must have stock in the power company … all the electricity they waste. Bet they have security cameras, as well, that they never look at. I could buy a fancy sports car with all the money they spend trying to feel safe, after advertising how much money they've got by lighting everything up.

If I'm in the mood for company while I walk, I go downtown. Can't go a block without some guy with a sign telling you a sad story, and then asking for money. After a while, you get to recognize the ones who scam people by begging for a living, the alcoholics who beg for money to buy a drink, and the folks down on their luck who really need help. You can get a good conversation from any of them, if you give them a dollar or two.

You must be careful walking downtown, though. Not only are there muggers, there are creatures of the night much deadlier. They seek out the weak to satisfy their demented desires. Some rape, some maim, and some kill … it's what they do.

There was this young lady walking home a little earlier tonight. Her make-up was all streaky, and her nose puffy and red from crying. She was suffering and I felt bad for her. As she hurried to get by me, I turned to her and spoke out, "Miss, are you okay? Did someone try to hurt you?"

The poor thing got all defensive and shot back, "Why, are you thinking of trying something?"

I smiled back and shook my head. "What in the world could this old woman do to you? I can barely walk. I just saw you crying and thought maybe you could use another woman to lend an ear, if talking would make you feel better."

She seemed surprised another person would care about her problems. After a moment, she smiled, but followed it immediately with a cascade of tears and a runny nose. Young lady broke down, right there on the sidewalk. I gently hugged her and let the tears flow for a few minutes. Finally getting control of herself, the both of us sat down on the curb and she started telling me all about her troubles.

"Jessica, my friend, set me up with this guy. He was supposed to be going to college and treat me with respect, according to her. Well, he picked me up and took me out to dinner. I found out he wasn't going to college, but thought he might, one day. Before we got out of the restaurant's parking lot, he started putting his hands all over me, like I'd given him permission to do whatever he wanted. When I stopped him, he got all mad and told me to get out of the car. I just moved here and don't have any idea where I'm at, or where I'm going. I grabbed the wrong purse and don't even have money for a cab. I hate Jessica, I hate that bastard, and I hate myself for moving here. I wish I was dead!"

I raised my arm for her to come over. She sat next to me and I cradled her close, with my arm gently over her shoulders, as she let loose with another outburst of tears. When I left, she had no more problems. Made me feel so good inside.

Moving on down the street, I headed for a section of town known for late night parties. My mind wandered to the days when my own daughter had gone out and chanced danger from the creatures of the night. She was so beautiful. Her hair had been so soft and blonde, like one of God's angels. Her smile could take away tears in a second. Watching her onstage at her graduation ceremonies had filled my heart with such joy and pride. Her speech, as class valedictorian, held the crowd silent and attentive in every way. Oh, what a speech it was— all about opportunities to change the world and such. That day is still so very special to my heart. Shame it ended so badly.

Popular, oh my God, she was so popular ... every boy wanted to date her. Graduation night, we had a nice dinner with a few relatives, and then she went out. I wanted her to stay home, but she said there was a graduation party taking place, and she wanted to see some of her classmates for the last time. So, I let her go. I was worried, not about her, but about some of the other kids. Graduation parties have a reputation, you know, and not a good one.

I stayed up late, waiting for her to come home. I sent her a text, but got no response. My nerves got the best of me and I had to take a walk to calm down. It was such a warm evening that when I got home, I took a bath. When she still wasn't home, I fixed a cup of decaf so I could sleep later, but dozed off before I finished it.

Around three in the morning, there was a knock at the door. I'd left it unlocked so she could get in without having to use her key—you know, if she wanted to get away from a boy trying to get more than she wanted to give—and opened it to see two police officers in front of me.

Oh, my heart sank. I've always been one to think the worst, and this time was no different. "You're here about my daughter?" I watched for their faces to show some emotion ... something to tell me she was still alive. "Well, don't just stand there. Tell me what you're here to tell me."

The tall one started, "I hate to be the one to give you this news, but..." Oh, he told me, he did, told me she was found dead. My darling daughter wouldn't show her smile to anyone, ever again. All the words she'd spoken in her speech had been for others to follow. Her days of pursuing dreams and making people happy were over.

She and her recent boyfriend had left the party around midnight. It's assumed that they decided to park along the side of the lake, over at the park, and do what kids do. I don't have to explain that to you, I'm sure. You're younger than I am. Their bodies had later been found by an officer that first thought they'd fallen asleep, and walked over to wake them. Guess he got sick after seeing the mess they were in. Someone had gone crazy with a knife. Somehow, they'd snuck up on the two and started swinging away. Sliced them all up, even their faces. The inside of the car was filled with blood. We even had to have a closed coffin funeral. Such a shame, such a shame.

Sorry, it's just the girl I left a little while ago reminded me so much of my daughter. It's hard to forget at times. So very hard.

Doesn't seem to be much going on over here tonight. Oh, wait a minute, there's a big guy over there. Almost missed seeing him. He's right between the hedge row and building. Oh my God, will you look at that. He must have been peeing and passed out. His dick's still hanging out. Not much to hang out. Tiny little thing—he could have put that back in, without any trouble. He must have been super-drunk and passed out before he finished. Excuse me, I need to help this poor man out. I'll be right back.

Okay, that's two I've been able to help tonight. Time to call it an evening and head home. Makes walking worth it, helping people, that is. I always do my best to help folks out. Most don't appreciate it. But if I know I helped them, I'm happy.

My daughter didn't appreciate anything I did. Oh, she liked that I donated to good causes, and always purchased everything her school clubs were selling, if I did it through her. She was ashamed of me, and never wanted me to attend any of her events. I snuck in and watched her from afar, when she was a cheerleader. If she'd have known, she'd have killed me. I had to do it. She was my daughter.

I wouldn't let her rest until she finally agreed to me attending her graduation ceremonies. But I had to promise her I wouldn't tell anyone who I was. I agreed, so I could watch, but it hurt so much not being able to tell others she was my daughter. Later, when the few relatives showed up at the house who hadn't disowned us, she let it be known that she didn't like the way I dressed or acted. Told everyone I was an embarrassment to them. That hurt me so much. She wouldn't even give me a kiss when she left the house for the last time.

Oh, I knew she would end up at the lake that night. She should have known I'd listen in on her telephone conversations. But she didn't care. She was Queen Bitch, and could do as she pleased. Well, I showed her. Stupid slut, she'd been giving her boyfriend a blow job when I walked up. I rammed the ice pick into the back of his head and poked it around, to make sure he would be die. I think she thought he was having an orgasm, with all the groaning he did. I was glad she did. It gave me time to get my knife out of my purse. She looked up, drool still around her lips, and saw the sharp blade only a few inches from her face. When she saw I was the one holding it, she looked like she was getting ready to cuss me out. I stopped that really quick.

Oh, and that girl tonight, just as stupid as my daughter. She should have known better than to trust what a friend told her. Why, she could have been raped. She never saw the knife enter her body. But she died too fast. It took away half the fun. Why, I've had them squirm and roll about for several minutes before dying. But, this one, well, I must have hit more than a nerve.

By the way, I took it easy on the big guy I saw. I only cut off a little of his penis. Trouble is, all he had was a little! I just wish I had been around to see his face when he came out of his drunken stupor.

Anyway, it's time for me to say "Good Night" to you. I just want to get home and get out of this girdle and dress. So much to do before I can get to bed. My wig has to have the blood washed out of it, this make-up is going to take forever to remove, and I really need to itch my balls.

"See you around!"

Victims

The church bells calling the congregation to mass were the last damn thing my pounding head needed. Yanking out the bells' clappers and wrapping them around the head of the bell ringer crossed my mind, but I hesitated, remembering I wasn't in the land of "Anything Goes". There was something about being in a place of Christian worship that always affected me in a bad way. Last time, it was nausea, and today, the headache. Nothing about being there made me comfortable—even my ass ached from the hard, wooden pew. I believe preachers ordered them intentionally, to make their congregations squirm in case their sermons failed to do so.

To be blunt, the place bored me to death. There was nothing there of any entertainment value. How much excitement is there in watching the young and old, skinny and fat, and everything in between, parade by in their Sunday best? I get so thrilled about the obligatory prayers, watching so many pantomiming the singing of hymns, and watching the egotistical feel they've done their duty to cement their place in society as upstanding, because they made an appearance. So many charades and games, all for the benefit of man, not God. Hypocrites bred of hypocrites, and preached to by hypocrites ... the life of Christians.

I wondered if I wasn't the only one in attendance who wasn't trying to fool anyone. I had no charade to play, no one to impress, and no God to fear. I was here for only one reason ... to find my next target.

Many would think I'd appreciate inhabiting a body of my own gender. Boring! Been there, done that—it's more fun to experiment. My eyes followed the jiggling butts of the women, as they made their way down the aisle in their loud and awkward high heels. Those damn things are a self-imposed torture. I will say, it does make one stand straighter. And, the position is great for men, as the ass cheeks stick out more for their inspection. I call it "the tease from a sleaze" demanded by the men who dictate women's fashion.

I glanced at the old clock on the wall and notice it's time for services to begin. Those still standing meandered toward their seats of habit, in their favorite pews, to ensure they'd be seen and accounted for. None of those inside interested me, as most were going to be familiar faces in Hell in a few years, anyway. That is, until a blur flashed by and rushed to a seat, two rows in front of me. Once my eyes rested on her, they refused to move away.

The woman was in her middle years, say thirty-five to forty-five, but looked younger. There were no sagging boobs or ass cheeks, so common in women her age. In fact, there were barely any signs of a wrinkle, unlike the Grand Canyon topography so many in her group had developed. Moderately dressed, she brightened up the scenery, but maintained a certain modesty. Even her perfume smelled the scent of freshness, and brought images of fresh-mowed grass, dandelions, and afternoons in the park.

What? You didn't expect demons to have such feelings? You forget, for every good, there is a bad. I love seeing good wherever I go. It means there is evil everywhere, as well! I'm always at home.

Anyway, I needed to see my target closer. I wanted to merge into her body, and feel the softness of her skin become mine. Yet, when she turned around (in response to my stare burning holes in the back of her head), her eyes were filled with pain and suffering. Their torture, and the evil it brought forth, filled my stomach with pride. So, evil was a part of her life, even to this day. She would make a good soul for my insatiable hunger to feed upon.

The minister's whining and droning went on and on. His message was the same I had heard for centuries—the same old crap meant to make people feel bad about themselves, and feed the donation plate to make amends. I blocked him out and diverted my attention back to the woman. She became an obsession, and I yearned to hear her stories of woe and suffering. It would help me to relax. Examples of mental and physical agony always do that for me.

With services finally over, I rushed to maneuver myself in position to talk to her. Darting around those gossiping about who had been absent from church, I managed to pass her by as she stopped to give the minister her obligatory good-bye. As she left him and drew near, I opened the outer door and waited until she was next to me before saying, "Ma'am, you look as if you're somewhat stressed. Excuse this old church-goer for asking, but do you need someone to talk to?"

Her eyes met mine and I took control. Her will was obviously weak, as it is with most females who desire to find someone with whom to share their woes, their tales of grief, the story of their life. She wanted my company, knowing not where it might lead. Yet, on her face fear appeared. There was something else, something hiding inside, something I had yet to see.

"Come with me. There's a coffee shop across the street. I am of no threat to you. I am simply a man who sees one suffering, and believes he might be of some service. Shall we?"

Over a steaming cup of caffeine, she stammered about and told me her sad tale. A recent widow, she described, with tears streaming down her cheeks, how her husband had been decapitated in an auto accident. She had been at home, dinner for two on the stove, dealing with her doctor's diagnosis of her never being able to have a child. When the phone rang and she received news of the tragedy, she'd sat down and let the food burn. There was no reason to rush to the hospital. He was dead, and nothing would bring him back. She was alone in the world, and in her grief. She was determined to stay that way.

As she spoke, I felt her will go back and forth. My control wavered, as she proved herself stronger than I had believed her to be. I was forced to play a role I'd played in the past, one of a caring ear and full of sympathy. I rose to go to the shop counter and get refills, bringing back some extra napkins to help dry her eyes. Seating myself next to her, I laid my hand gently upon her shoulder, in a caring gesture. She smiled and took a sip of the hot coffee, grabbing at a napkin as a drop drooled down her chin.

Her story continued, with her worries about money. Monthly bills were going unpaid, as her husband's assets were locked because of his death. She feared losing her job as she had taken extra days off to deal with the funeral and all her problems. Now, there was the potential of losing her job, and becoming homeless.

Her agony was so enlightening, especially after having sat through church. My faith in evil was restored once more. Yet, I had to be careful not to show my joy. I still needed to make her feel completely safe with me. So, I used words to comfort her—things a friend would say during a time of suffering. I really am a ham, when it comes to that. Next, I asked her to make a list when she got home, of all the creditors and their phone numbers, and call them on Monday. I gave her directions on what to say to get them to extend her billing period, in a time of personal tragedy.

I continued with my own sad story, concocted on the spot. I told her I had recently lost my wife to cancer, and of my struggles since. I manufactured tears to prey upon her emotions, and build a bond of us both having suffered loss. The story I made up was a true masterpiece, if I say so myself. The extra napkins I had brought back were gone quickly, as both her and I used them up.

Feeling the connection was made, I stated I needed to run some errands, but would like to see her the next evening ... as a friend ... if she would allow me to do so. I realized I was taking a chance. We had only just met, and she could have turned me away. My storytelling ego got a boost when her eyes lit up and, with a slight smile, she whispered, "That would be nice."

She gave me her phone number without hesitation. It was now time for my final touch. "I am going to give you something. You will probably try to refuse it, but I won't let you. I would never offer this to a stranger, if I didn't feel they were in dire need."

From my pocket, I pulled a crisp, sealed envelope, and placed it on the table in front of her. I always keep one handy, in case of an unexpected meeting, much like ours today. Before she could open it, I rose and left her with my gift.

The next afternoon, I called to make sure she hadn't decided to back out of our dinner engagement. Her mood had changed from sadness to happiness, and her gratitude was in grand supply. It almost made me sick, she'd lost all that grand pain and suffering stuff I loved.

You know what's pathetic? The love of money is a sin, yet, I've never seen a minister turn away an offering plate. Obviously, the girl was of the same mold. The three thousand dollars in the envelope had "saved" her, and she believed it to be a gift from God. How quickly she'd forgotten I had given it to her. I did have a difficult time holding back my laughter when she said that, though. She would have freaked if she had known it came from Hell, instead.

Arriving at her house, she rushed out and greeted me before I could get out of my car. Her modest look from Sunday had changed into one of "it's date night." Her low-cut dress gave me more than an idea of what she had to offer, and her make-up had taken hours to perfect. She wanted to impress … and she did. The body I inhabited had become old and rundown, but a spark of life lit up urges to explore not felt in years. There was no doubt, the night would become an adventure.

Our drive to the restaurant was filled with the overindulgence of gratitude being exhibited. She'd been able to pay many of her bills, and thanks to my advice, other creditors had made concessions to due dates, in lieu of the forthcoming insurance payoff. All of this had happened because God had brought me to her, in her mind. I could hardly keep a straight face.

Sitting around a candle-lit table, the sweet sounds of Italy played softly over the speakers. I'd visited the place several times over the decades, and had always been satisfied. We chatted about our likes and dislikes, without making it sound like a question and answer period, while enjoying a large salad. To her, it was nothing more that getting to know each other. To me, well, I needed to know if she would be a compatible host to live within.

Eventually, the conversation made a left turn, into the topic of her current status. Waiting to get married until she was established in the business world, she and her husband had enjoyed speed boats, hiking, and evenings filled with wine and dancing. She loved experimenting with food recipes, and lived for the excitement that diversity provided. She preferred reading over television, basketball over football, and adventure over routine. With a bucket list including hot air ballooning and visiting Rio, her zest for life was enticing.

After-dinner drink glasses empty, she suggested we keep the evening going. With the bright moon lighting up the sky, we headed for the nightclub district of the downtown area. Side by side, we walked through the streets, passing by the clubs, instead preferring private conversation. I was the hunter, but found myself being hunted by my prey. She was intoxicating, her humor and wit drawing me in and negating the power of my defenses. Instead of being timid about being seen with an older man, she appeared to relish in the fact she was with one—as if the prize was, indeed, hers for all to see. The spell she cast over me boosted my ego, as I considered her my prize, as well. Yet, the sight of another young/old couple reminded me of the things money could purchase. I shook my head, knowing I had paid well for our time together. Perhaps I'd been naïve in thinking her attracted to the skin I wore. I was nothing more than a sugar daddy to her. As the night came to an end, I would need to take control of her will, once more, to collect the change she'd forgotten to return.

But this woman was good, seriously, one of the best. She was able to pull me back and reconsider my thoughts, by feigning weakness. She removed her heels, displaying how they had blistered her tender toes and heel. As we turned to go to my car, she began walking as if each step put her in agony. I fed well off her misery, but volunteered to bring the car back to her, if she wouldn't mind waiting a few minutes. I could see her considering my offer, but eventually it was turned down, for her fear of being left alone. Soon, I found her arm draped upon my neck and shoulder, to reduce the weight put on her feet and lessen the pain of her steps. Her body felt natural against mine, as if it was meant to be there. The bumping of our hips as we walked set a rhythm I hoped would intensify as the evening progressed.

The drive back to her house made me long for the days of bench seats in cars. Her body leaned across the center console around corners, even though I was taking them slow. It was easy to see she had enjoyed the feeling of our bodies next to each other as much as I.

Of course, her invite for one last drink to end the evening was accepted. My control had nothing to do with it. The drink was all her idea. Again, I'd done well, and patted myself on the back.

As she closed the door behind me, the click of the deadbolt locking told me I wouldn't be leaving soon.

No, there was no drink, unless one considers the swapping of spit a new concoction for bartenders to prepare. She became a tigress in need, her arms wrapped around my neck, refusing to let go. Her lips, so hungry, but tender, met mine and exploded my brain with memories of a younger life, and a time filled with hot passion. Forcing me against a wall, her firm breasts pressed deep into my chest and left permanent impressions as she raised one leg up and around the back of mine, so our lower bodies could touch and add to the fire building.

I felt like a teenager all over again!

In her fervor, she pulled back, yanking and pulling to remove my jacket and shirt. Her fingers fought to free my belt and undo my slacks, finally probing under my shorts until they located the passionate fire she had raised.

All the time she was on the attack, I was battling inside the body she sought for pleasure. Yes, as a demon, I wanted to merge with her, to become one and leave this old man's body, to enjoy the younger one of hers. Yet, she had driven my desires to extremes not realized for decades. I needed to experience the pleasures she held, at least one time, before merging. I had to have her as a man, if for nothing more, so I could have a memory of what it felt like for the opposite sex, when I took over her body and returned to my natural gender, a woman, once again.

The she-tiger was relentless. Her eyes, now filled only with lust, burned into my skull, and we intertwined. Leaving her clothes upon the hallway floor, she pulled me into the bedroom and finished disrobing me in seconds. She pushed me back upon the bed and climbed on top, immediately mounting me and beginning her ride, our exchange of passion.

My plans to merge took a backseat to the moment I wanted to never forget. Yet the energy she exhibited enveloped me, and drove our quest for the ultimate peak, much sooner than desired. I recognized the feeling of my head exploding and, quivering with satisfaction, was coming. Yes, this woman, this power machine, was the person I had to become. Her ability to drive a man crazy was beyond any I'd ever encountered. Merging into her meant years of moments like these. But, instead of being on the bottom, I'd be the one driving the energy forward, on top.

Unable to hold back another second, I released. Yet, my bucking and jerking wasn't normal. I was being pulled inside of her, literally. It wasn't I doing the merging, this time. Looking down at me, the passion she'd shown was gone. Now, a look of determination had replaced the sexual intensity. The more I felt myself losing the body I'd inhabited, the brighter her eyes glowed green. I had an epiphany. This wasn't a woman, not a normal one. This was another demon, doing her thing, absorbing my life's energy instead of merging.

I fought back, attempting to neutralize her attempt. I refused to yield to her and screamed, "No, you're making a mistake. It is I who am to control the body, not another demon of possession! I cannot allow you to possess me as you would a human."

The room filled with her maniacal laughter as the walls bulged, and the ceiling plaster cracked, from the energy our battle loosed. But she had gotten the upper hand on me, and my passion had allowed that to happen. As my energy ebbed, I began to see through her eyes. I had lost, evident as the old man's body withered away, becoming rotting skin atop a skeleton between my legs. I could sense the satisfaction of another, present inside. Its joy was as strong as my disgust.

It was then I heard the voice of the one who had defeated me. "You were easy to defeat. Feel no sorrow in losing. I have been around for centuries and you are just a pup, in comparison. Accept defeat and join me, as we will enjoy all life has to offer. For years I have sought a female to be my constant companion. A strong couple we shall make, you and me. If we find our time together unacceptable, we can always part into separate hosts, at that time."

Together, we have roamed for many years. We have found a greater strength as one, a strength none have been successful in defeating. We enjoy what we have, while we have it. Yet, we have discovered our host body ages much faster, with both of us feeding upon it. If we are to remain as one, we must hunt much more frequently ... or starve. So, we prowl, seeking our next.

You may wonder who we have chosen. Beware, as only time will tell.

The Curse

Watching the German Shepherd wolf down his food made me feel all good inside. Although I knew better, he attacked his bowl of dry food as if he hadn't eaten in days. Didn't take him long to finish. I'd barely set it down and returned inside, when he was munching on the last of it. Terri, my wife, stood beside me, witnessing his completion of the feast. "Looks like we got ourselves a dog, doesn't it?"

"I took a chance on buying the twenty-five-pound bag of food earlier today, figuring it would come back again for dinner. I'm wondering where he spends his day, though?" The animal finished licking the bowl and glanced up at me, his huge tongue hanging out of his mouth. I had no doubt he knew we were talking about him, and didn't care, if his stomach was kept full. Satisfied, he took a couple of steps, curled himself up atop the blanket I had laid out for him, and fell into a deep sleep. Yeah, we'd gotten ourselves a dog.

I thought back, two days before, when he had first shown up at our back door. Terri, somewhat skittish of larger animals, had first seen him while cooking dinner. She'd let out a shriek and hollered for me to come take a look. Outside the door he sat, as if he'd been invited and was awaiting someone to answer the door and let him in. Not a pup, by any means, he had to be at least a year or two old, maybe more, and with feet so big he was bound to grow much larger. Skinny as a greyhound, his bones protruded beneath his black and gray coat of matted fur—dirty and full of fleas. His huge head and mouth, full of large, yellowish teeth, made him a formidable opponent, should someone decide to challenge him. Thankfully, he displayed no signs of being outwardly aggressive. Even so, neither of us were anxious to open the wooden door and take a chance on him crashing through the screen one, to make us his next meal.

Not expecting our guest, we hadn't prepared a meal in his honor. We talked about shooing him away, but neither of us wanted to insult his integrity, and make him mad. Thinking fast, I recommended we feed him the leftover meatloaf Terri had sitting in the fridge, from a few days before. Reluctant, but without another option, she conceded, but not without first giving me the over the eye glasses, "I hate you forever" look she had patented in Washington, D.C.

On the counter sat my enemy. Ever since I'd gagged my way through its initial appearance at the dinner table, I'd been trying to find a way to not face it again, hoping, instead, it would spoil quickly and have to be thrown out. Once in a great while, Terri made a mistake and her meatloaf was edible. This one had not fallen into that category. Careful not to allow any of the dreaded goo to get on me, I tipped the plate and watched as it released itself from the airplane-glue grip of cold grease holding it in place. Finally, it sat on its new paper plate home, and was ready to be disposed of in charity to the Animal Kingdom. It didn't have the formality one of my wife's

China plates would have had, but it would keep me from having to clean it up off the back porch, should the animal recognize it to be an unsatisfactory meal, as I had found previously.

There was excitement building inside me. Biting my tongue, so as not to exhibit my elation at not having to choke it down myself, I walked back to the door and peered through the glass. Our guest was still in the same position, his head cocked to the side, as if saying, "Hey, I'm waiting. Are you about ready to serve, or do I need to check out another restaurant?"

A little voice in my head started saying, "He's going to take one look at that crap and decide to eat you, instead." Knowing that a valid possibility, I gathered my courage and stepped outside with the sacrificial meatloaf. Words of confidence roared through my brain, reassuring my act be recognized as one of good will as I set the plate down, a few feet in front of the dog. "No, you're not going to bite. You're a good dog. Don't prove me wrong and take off my hand, you bastard. Just stay where you're at. Dinner is served."

My bravery astounded me. I was amazed at how desperate I was to avoid eating the food myself, and the chances I'd take to accomplish that. Food in place, I backed away and took shelter from any attack behind the screen door.

The German Shepherd stayed seated. I couldn't tell if he was wondering if it was okay to begin, awaiting permission to start, or questioning if Terri's meatloaf was worth the effort. Finally, he rose to all fours, advanced a couple of steps closer, and took a whiff of the wonderful blend of hamburger, onion, catsup, and her own mixture of special and secret seasonings. After a few seconds of hesitation, he began nibbling at it. A bite or two later, he started tearing off larger pieces to swallow, until the loaf of dread was gone. Licking his jaws and mouth, he returned to his sitting position and, again cocking his head, gave me another look. Terri giggled, thinking he'd shown me it was good. But I knew better. His look was one that said, "If this was a restaurant, you'd have an empty parking lot. I saved your butt tonight, but don't force me to do it tomorrow. You owe me!"

He was gone when I left for work yesterday morning. Thinking he might not return, possibly ill (hopefully not dying) from the meatloaf, I stopped at the store on the way home, and only bought a small box of dog food. If he had survived, I wanted to be ready.

All the way home, I anticipated him being there, waiting. I guess I'd already accepted him as our dog, and formed a bond of some sort. The disappointment I had when Terri told me she hadn't seen him all day hit me harder than I'd expected. I wasn't ready for the kinship between us being erased. It put a damper on my day. So much for being my best buddy. Saddened, the horror of the fate of Terri's future meatloaf leftovers slid (on its own grease) into my thoughts. I shuddered at the thought of what I might have to go through in the months, even years, ahead. I believe Terri recognized my grief—and enjoyed seeing me suffer. I'm sure she felt a sort of justice had been served.

As we began our dinner, we were interrupted by a scratching at the back screen. A grand smile crossed my face as I saw our acquaintance, again sitting where he had been twenty-four hours before. I grabbed the dog food, emptied it into my favorite popcorn bowl, and rushed it to him. He examined the food, raised his head, and blinked his approval, before beginning his devouring of all I'd given. I was amazed at how fast he engulfed it—twice as fast as he'd eaten the meatloaf the night before! (This fact I reminded Terri of repeatedly over the course of the evening, just because I could.)

Don't get me wrong, I love Terri. We've only been married about six months, but she's the best thing that ever happened to me. We met and immediately clicked. Two months later, we tied the knot, much to the chagrin of her parents—both claiming we needed to give it more time and get to know each other better. There was no need. Our sarcasm, humor, and future dreams meshed perfectly. And, in bed, she was a sex goddess. My job stressed me out and exhausted me, so the weeknight episodes were far and few between. But the weekends— God, I lived for them. We'd stay in bed most of Saturday, and all of Sunday, except when she did the weekly grocery shopping. Of course, like all women, there were times she refused me—usually once a month.

Those times of the curse were torture. Still, I found ways to survive them.

Anyway, as I stated earlier, I stopped and purchased a large bag of dog food before coming home. I also made the investment in two chrome bowls, one each, for food and water. You should have seen his excitement when I sat them down in front of him. The German Shepherd seemed so proud. He accepted them as a "Welcome to your new home" type of statement. And, when he saw the ugly blanket I'd pulled from the closet and situated on the porch for him to sleep upon, he knew he had become a third member of the household.

"So, you seem happy to have a dog," Terri whispered as she lay beside me in bed later. "You've given him food, bowls, and my grandmother's blanket I inherited. Don't worry, I didn't like it, either. He eats here and spends the night, but he's gone every afternoon. Where do you think he goes?"

"I had wondered the same thing," I replied, hating to tell her what I'd discovered. "There is a carnival in town, over at the fairgrounds. That's just a few blocks away. I'm betting he belongs to one of the workers there. He probably hangs around with him during the day, and when the carnival starts up in the evening, he comes here to get some decent food. I had considered buying some dog shampoo and a flea collar, but figured it better to wait and see if he leaves us when the carnival closes Saturday night. I really want him to stay, but if he doesn't, there is nothing we can do."

Sighing, Terri expressed her disappointment. "Yeah, that makes sense. I want him to stay, as well. I hate to think of him not being around. Who else will eat my leftover meatloaf?"

A chuckle started out, but was cut off by her fingers jabbing my ribcage. I was going to continue the sarcasm contest by saying, "The dog really doesn't like it, either", but decided it best to remain quiet and get some sleep in the bed, instead of trying to get comfortable on the couch.

The next afternoon, Terri was sitting on the living room couch, immersed in her task of figuring out how to have Jeffrey rearrange the front two rooms over the weekend. The battle to fit things properly was almost as bad as the one she knew she'd have getting him out of bed to do it. She appreciated the attention, but his need for sex bordered upon addiction.

Three months ago, he'd hurt his back trying to move the furniture alone, while she'd been shopping. That one had been planned on the week of her monthly period, so he couldn't use sex for an excuse. She had returned home to find nothing had been moved, and him claiming back pain. This time, they'd do it together on Saturday afternoon, and use a floor plan to eliminate unnecessary rearranging. No excuses.

On the cusp of deciding where to locate the sofa and love seat, her thoughts were interrupted by a loud rapping at the front door. Opening it, she found two police officers waiting.

"Sorry to disturb you, ma'am, but we're investigating the disappearance of a carnival worker, a young lady. Have you seen any strangers in the neighborhood lately?"

"Besides my husband?" she retorted with a smile, hoping her sarcasm would be appreciated. They gave no indication it was. Straightening up, she continued, "No, officer, I haven't.

"Then, do you recognize the person in this photo?" The smaller, silent officer held up a picture of a woman in her mid-twenties. She was standing in front of a cotton candy trailer, in cut-off jeans accentuating the legs Terri wished she had, and a tight tank top that did nothing to hide the rigid nipples beneath it. *Yeah, typical carnival trash.* Still, the woman seemed familiar, as if she had been seen. Stumped, Terri told the two she hadn't seen her, and wished them good luck in their search.

Going back to tackling the floor plan, Terri tried to concentrate, but couldn't get the picture out of her mind. She knew she'd seen the girl ... but where? The boxes on the floor plan began to change, resembling houses on their street. She pictured hers at the end, and moved down a few. *There, that's where I saw her! I was leaving the house to go shopping, last Sunday afternoon, and she was walking down the street. I drove right by her!*

Rushing outside, she failed to locate the officers. Standing at the end of the drive, she debated on calling the station to have them return. *I should tell them what I*

215

know, but I don't really know anything. I only saw her once, and that was on Sunday, days ago. Others had to have seen her walking in the area. I'm sure they already know that. No need in wasting their time.

Returning inside, she completed the floor plan and prepared dinner. Tonight would be Jeffrey's favorite, chicken breasts stuffed with a Mexican mix and baked in three types of cheese. He arrived late, apologized, and they began to eat immediately. Between bites, he asked, "So, should we wait another couple of days to see if the dog stays, or should we go ahead and name him?"

Damn him, he always does that ... wait until I've got a mouthful before asking me a question. It's some sort of damn game to him. "So, are you practicing to apply for a job as a waiter, or does it make you happy to see me swallow half-chewed food in order to answer you?"

"Whoa, Kemosabe, I just asked you a question. No need to go spastic over it. Take your time and answer when you want. I'll be here all evening."

"I'm sorry," Terri sighed, somewhat apologetic for the outburst. "In answer to your question, I don't know. Let's wait, I guess. If we give him a name, we'll get even more attached, and it will hurt more if he does leave when the carnival goes."

"That was my feeling, too," Jeffrey responded, his mouth half-filled with mashed potatoes. "I do like the dog. He was here when I left for work this morning. Must have stayed all night. And, he was here when I got home tonight. I was late, but he was early. Maybe, we'll luck out and he'll decide to stay, instead of leaving when the carnival does. He definitely is getting better fed here."

"Oh, speaking of the carnival, a couple of police officers stopped in earlier today," she began, wondering if she should stick the piece of chicken on her fork in her mouth, to make him wait, or finish telling him first. "They were looking for a missing woman from the carnival. It's the strangest thing, I didn't remember where I'd seen her until after they'd left. She was walking down the street Sunday, when I went shopping. I remember you sulking about me being on my period, I'm sorry, you were working in the garden. I drove by her, a couple of houses down. I almost called them back, but I didn't. I figured someone else had seen her and already reported it. She didn't stop here, did she?"

Jeffrey nearly choked. "No, didn't see her. Like you said, I was working in the garden—not sulking. She probably just walked on by. Who knows? So, you didn't tell them anything, right?"

"Oh, you were sulking. No, I didn't tell them a thing. Do you think I should have?"

Struggling to swallow, Jeffrey took a drink of iced tea to wash down the overcooked chicken before answering. "No, you did just fine. No need in bothering them. No need at all."

Terri's Friday morning began like any other. A quick toaster pastry and coffee with Jeffrey, sticking dirty clothes in the washer, and a ritualistic changing of the

217

sheets on the bed, in preparation for their weekend together. Tucking the fitted corners under the mattress, she found herself getting excited, anticipating the next two days filled with torrid lovemaking ... minus a couple of hours to move furniture. Maybe she was the sex addict. Jeffrey was always too tired during the week, but the weekends were their time together. This one would be special. The weekends after her monthly curse always were. Jeffrey hadn't been happy, but she didn't feel right doing anything when her body was cleansing itself. It was a part of life he'd have to get used to. There wasn't anything she could do to change it. But this weekend would make up for it. She'd make sure of that!

The bed fresh and ready for action, she returned to the kitchen to finish off the last of the coffee in the pot. Extra creamer and sugar were always needed to counter the taste of a two-hour old pot. As she lifted the cup to take a sip, the phone rang. Answering, Terri heard only the silence of a dead line. Seconds after putting down the phone, it rang again. As she lifted it to her ear, she realized the voice on the other end had already begun to speak. "... and be sure to ask your husband how he liked my boob tattoos. He seemed to enjoy chewing on them last Sunday. He kept saying, 'Maria, these taste like cotton candy'."

And, the voice was gone.

Terri barely made it to the chair, before collapsing. *Who in the hell was that? Sunday? Jeffrey was home Sunday. He didn't go anywhere, he couldn't have met up with someone. We were together most of the day. I was only gone an hour or two. I know he was working in the garden. He was soaked with sweat when I got back. This must be bullshit. Someone's jealous of what he and I have together. They just want us to get a divorce, so they can move in on him. Either that, or it's a sorry excuse for a joke!*

That afternoon was anything but peaceful. In her mind, Terri analyzed last Sunday every five minutes, desperately seeking any time that Jeffrey could have played around on her. And, who the hell was this woman named Maria ... some hot Latin lover with cotton candy tits? When did she come into the picture? Did she work with her husband, know him from before they'd been married, or what? Between breaking a couple of dishes as she got them out of the dishwasher, and fits of tears and depression, Terri was a mess.

That evening, the German Shepherd was fed, as usual, but the food on the table remained untouched. Terri's attack had come fast and furious, before the first bite had been taken. Questions, accusations, explanations—all were tossed back and forth, without concern of the anger being shot forth. Both said many things to hurt the other as frustrations grew. Jeffrey's denials made sense, and fit her logical thoughts, but the mysterious phone call drove her emotions. Finally, she had nothing left to say. She had no evidence of any wrongdoing, only a weird phone call to base it on. Logic dictated Jeffrey was innocent, not guilty as charged. Still feeling detached from him, they went to bed and tried to sleep. Jeffrey did so with no problem. Terri's brain couldn't shut down. The weekend wasn't going as expected.

Rising Sunday morning, Terri decided to make a special breakfast for Jeffrey. He'd been especially caring all day Saturday, trying to help her get the phone call out of her mind and make things between them right. His multiple performances in bed, and his willingness to rearrange the living room, had more than made up for any lingering doubts. With the coffee brewing and the bacon spattering, she prepared the pancake mix.

Maybe today, I can find a way to keep him out of the garden, and busy elsewhere. It's going to be too hot and humid to work outside, anyway. The breeze through the window isn't even cooling off the kitchen right now. Time to get him complaining about high utility bills and turn on the air conditioning. I'll give him a reason to appreciate it later.

But first, breakfast was almost ready. Time to wake him.

Turning down the cooking bacon, Terri hurried to the bedroom, jumped on her side of the bed, and nearly sent Jeffrey flying off the other side. Completely lost in what was happening, he grabbed at the mattress to hold on. "Get up, sleepy head," Terri's voice rang out. "I've got breakfast almost ready. You'll need a full stomach to keep up with me the rest of the day."

Giggling, she managed to slip off the bed and reach the door, before Jeffrey could retaliate.

Arriving in the kitchen, she turned the bacon back up and heated up the griddle for the pancakes. As she was ready to pour the first one out, she caught a glimpse of two men coming around the side of the house and up the back steps. Both dressed in dirty T-shirts and jeans, she knew they had to be from the carnival ... probably coming after the dog. Then it hit her. She'd opened the main door and left only the screen door between her and the outside, trying to get a breeze to cool things off.

She rushed to the door, but they were already there.

"See, I told you. I knew I'd spotted him over here, when I was driving around the other morning. Not a lot of dogs look like him. Seems like he's found a new home."

"What are you two doing in my yard?" Terri demanded through the screen. "You do realize you're on private property, don't you?"

"We were just wondering about the dog, ma'am. We know his owner. Is Maria here?"

There was that name again ... Maria. The one with the tattooed boobs ... the one who had called.

"No, there's no Maria here. Now leave, before I call the police. You're trespassing."

Watching to ensure they left, Terri stormed back to find the bacon burned in the skillet. Fighting the strips to get them into the trash, her telephone began ringing. Half listening, she stuck it up to her ear.

"I'm here. I never left." It was the same voice as before … Maria's. Stunned, she turned off the stove and sat down at the table.

This is too much. The phone calls, the two guys from the carnival, the dog … what the hell is going on?

"I heard the phone. Who called?"

All the emotions from Friday flooded back. "Oh, I was going to fix you breakfast and then fuck your brains out, but two guys, probably carnival workers, just walked right around the back of the house and recognized the dog as Maria's. Then, after I got rid of them and burned the damn bacon, guess who calls? Yeah, Maria … good old Maria. Oh, she said she never left, by the way. Where the hell is she, in the damn basement? What is going on? Tell me! And don't you dare lie. Did you fuck her? I want to know!"

Caught off guard, Jeffrey raised up his hands, to ward against the onslaught. "Terri, I told you, I don't know anyone named Maria. I don't know what's going on … it's weird, for sure. And, we both knew the dog probably belonged to someone from the carnival. You know carnival people, they're always scamming people. She probably set this whole thing up to scam us out of money, possibly by claiming we stole the dog. Who knows?"

"Then, how did she get my phone number?"

"I have no idea," he spat back at her question. "I don't know, and to be honest, I don't give a damn. If you can't believe me, then the hell with you. I'm innocent.

Why would I jeopardize everything we've got and lie? It makes no sense. If you'd think about it, you'd see it doesn't. I'm going to take a shower and try to wake up. Save me some coffee. I'll need it."

Terri's mind flip-flopped between guilty and innocent. *He makes sense, but nothing else does. I don't know if I'm coming or going. C'mon, Terri, get yourself together. Things will be okay. Toughen up and make your man some breakfast.*

Laying another batch of bacon in the skillet, she tried to stop the tears and regain control of her emotions. The pancake griddle had warmed up and was ready. Reaching for the batter, she stopped when a loud rapping sounded from the front door. Moving the bacon skillet to a cold burner, she groaned, "Who in the hell is that, now? If it's a woman named Maria, I'm gonna scream."

In the doorway stood the same two officers she'd seen Friday. "Ma'am, we need to talk to you and your husband. We've received some new information that needs to be sorted out. Would you get him for us, please?"

"If this is about the carnival workers, they were trespassing. And, the dog was half-starved when it got here. We didn't steal it, we've just been feeding the poor thing."

"I'm here, officer." A soaking wet Jeffrey appeared, wearing the bottoms of a sweat suit and flip-flops. "Excuse my appearance. I just got out of the shower. What's this all about?"

Before either officer could answer, the German Shepherd rounded the corner of the house and trotted toward them. Fearing an attack, they reached for their pistols, but stopped when the dog sat down a few feet away. Barking a couple of times, the dog motioned his head as if to say, "Follow me." He then stood up and started to the side of the house, barking at them again.

The two looked at each other and shrugged. Leaving the smaller one at the door, the other followed the dog to the edge of the house and around to the backyard. After a few minutes, he returned to the door. "Folks, you need to come with us. This may be something we all need to see."

The walk from the front to the back yard was surreal to Terri. It was as if she were outside her body, looking down at the group. The officers, following the couple, were the executioners, only waiting for the command to kill. Yet, she'd done nothing. Why was the ominous cloud hanging over her head?

The German Shepherd was digging frantically in the garden. All watched as his huge paws scooped out vast amounts of dirt, without hesitation. No loose dirt escaped his efforts. He kept digging and digging, until only the hind legs and tail were visible. Then, he ceased, pushed himself back out of the hole, and turned to the group, barking over and over.

As the larger officer approached the hole and took a long look at the bottom, the dog backed off and sat down. Without saying a word, the officer returned to the group and restrained Jeffrey in handcuffs first, and then Terri.

"What's there, Jeffrey? What's there?" she screamed, all emotions coming to a head. "What did you do? What, Jeffrey, what?"

She couldn't believe it when he dropped his gaze to the ground, refusing to meet her eyes. "What have you done, Jeffrey? What lies have you told me? Where does the truth start and the lies end? Our making love over and over—was it only a ploy to fool me into thinking you were innocent?"

Terri's head spinning, she was no longer able to stand. Her knees buckled, and she dropped to the ground. Falling forward, the blades of grass pricked at her face as she continued screaming the same questions, but receiving no answers. She wanted to know ... needed to know ... had to know what was in the hole. She didn't want the visions coming to the forefront of her imagination. She wanted the truth. Her head swimming, stress overcame her, and her body relaxed into the darkness.

Had Terri truly been outside looking in, she would have seen the German Shepherd standing over her, doing his best to lick her face. He was tired of the pain his owners had endured, and weary of having to find new ones with which to share his love.

Coming to, Terri took a few minutes to shake the cobwebs and realize she was being hospitalized. Over to the side of the room sat her parents. It hit her that she must have been out for quite a while, if they had driven in from way out of town and were sitting by her side. "Mama, what happened? What did the police find?"

Her father stood and aided her mother in rising from the chair and going to her bedside, before beginning. Reaching over to rest his hand on her forearm, he whispered, "Honey, maybe you should wait a while before hearing about it."

"Hush, Daddy. Mama, I want to know. What did the police find?"

Tears glistened in her mother's eyes. Struggling to keep her voice calm, she began. "Baby girl, they found bodies … lots of bodies. Four, maybe five or six, they don't know yet, until they put all the parts together. Jeffrey had been killing one a month, ever since you two had been married. He was crying so hard as he confessed, they said. Crying because he did it to keep them quiet. He didn't want you to know he had raped them. He said he loved you, and didn't want to lose you. Some of what he said didn't make any sense. He kept repeating he did it because of the curse. No one knows what curse he's talking about. It all sounds so crazy, but he'd have to be crazy to do such horrible things. He's in jail, and won't be getting out for a long time, if ever. We're so blessed, Baby Girl, so blessed you're okay. If it hadn't been for that dog, you might have ended up being murdered by him, too. It was only a matter of time."

Lying back, Terri began to laugh. Easy at first, then louder, until it grew into the maniacal laughter of a crazed person. Her parents held each other close, frightened and worried—their daughter in such a state—as a nurse administered a sedative.

It's hilarious, but no one gets it but me. Jeffrey isn't crazy, he's a sex maniac. He's addicted to screwing, having his weekend nookie, his end of the week dessert. He couldn't go one weekend a month without it. It's terrible, but so damn funny. Yeah, there's a curse—every woman's curse—the once a month curse. The son-of-a-bitch couldn't handle it! There's no telling what he would have done to the dog if we'd have had it longer! Now, he'll get all the sex he wants, in prison. I hope he gets it every night, right up the ass.

The sedatives began to take hold. Her laughter died down and her eyes wouldn't stay open. *Thank God I didn't get pregnant. He would have killed and killed, waiting on the baby to be born and me to heal. What a sick bastard!*

Forty miles away, a young German Shepherd rode along the highway, with his head sticking out the window of a pick-up truck. His tongue, hanging out the side of his mouth, tasted the wind and all it offered. Somewhere, he would find a home with normal people. He'd leave the carnival life and settle down. He'd search until he found the right owners ... ones who loved and treated all with respect ... ones who didn't feed him leftover meatloaf or cotton candy.

Neighborhood Watch(er)

How dare you call me a "Peeping Tom". That, my friend, is an insult to my professionalism. I don't peep, I observe. If I were to receive stimulation or gratification from what I viewed, then you could assign me that title. Until you can prove that to be the case, I demand you cease the name calling.

Oh, there are those who are fitting of being called a Peeping Tom. Many are perverse in their thoughts, stimulated by witnessing sexual acts, or preying upon the sight of others by invading the privacy of their homes, in hopes of heightening their own sexual fantasies. They may recall their victims when in private, to increase their own sexual pleasures, or may even do so while peeping. These are individuals in need of therapy. Although somewhat harmless, they have been known to step over the line into obsession, and become a danger to both their victims and themselves.

I am not one of them.

There is no increase in my sexual desires, by watching. In fact, I must say, I am embarrassed by much of what I see. No, my purpose in peering into windows is to ensure harmony is being maintained, and all are being treated with love and respect by those with whom they reside. It is my duty, my responsibility, my reason to live.

I am simply obeying the voices in my head.

See, the weak have no one to go to for assistance. Oh, there are shelters for some, but the initial act of leaving the home can be a dangerous event. Tempers can flare, words shouted in anger, and before you know it, someone lies either injured or dead. Picking up the phone and calling the police is usually a useless act, as well. Instead of doing their jobs, many officers consider themselves "peacemakers", and do nothing to the aggressor. The weak are left to those who know no mercy … only violence.

That is why I observe. That is why I act.

I walk the streets in the dark of night, usually during the spring and early fall, when the weather is cool and windows are open to the fresh air. My steps are soft, and my ears attuned to heated verbal battles and the screams of the helpless. No, I do not report them when heard. Instead, I make note of the address and return, time and time again, to see if it was a one-time incident or a habitual abuser. I follow those who reside in those homes into stores, where I might get close and see if they exhibit bruises, or other signs of physical mistreatment.

It is the voices that tell me when to get involved. Upon their command, I follow the offender, to become familiar with their routine. I scout out places they visit, and look for areas in which they could be taken easily. Man or woman, it matters not. Both have been guilty in the past. Neither sex is superior—both have been as evil as the other. These abusers must pay for their unacceptable behavior, and the tears they have brought. Their actions must not spread—especially to the children—and create abusive clones in the future.

Tonight, the one I watch staggers from the bar he visits before heading home. He crosses the center line of the street many times as he weaves through his neighborhood, narrowly missing several bike riders and a minivan as he ignores a stop sign and speeds through the intersection. I park my car and jog into his yard, listening to his shouting. Through the gap in the curtains, I see him slap his wife and knock her to the floor. She shouts back and receives another slap. Trying to rise to her feet, his kick to her ribcage puts her down on her side, gasping for air. Two young boys hurry down the stairs and rush to her aid, both being yanked away and beaten, before being made to sit on the couch. There, he drunkenly lectures them on how to become men, and quit being babies.

The voices tell me he is next on my list. I look forward to it.

A few nights later, I sit in a bar watching the man drink beer after beer. Other customers try to ignore his loud comments during a baseball game on television—most crude and inaccurate. His tendency to be in control and intimidate creates a tension among the patrons. Many move to tables away from the man, or leave the establishment entirely. He is told to leave several times, by those in attendance, but sneers at their demands.

There are none present to push him to violence—none large enough to win the battle. I am happy to see that is the case. I have plans.

The game ends and the man is told to leave by the bartender, already in the process of phoning the authorities. Only by the threat of spending a night in jail for public intoxication, does he exit—protesting to all those sitting along his route to the door. An applause fills the place when his departure is finally completed.

I follow after a few seconds, allowing for the attention of the patrons to go back to each other, instead of at my hurried exit. Many may be questioned later, by the authorities. I need to remain as anonymous as possible to avoid suspicion. I enter the parking lot and see the police have already arrived and have him in a discussion. He is telling them he is okay to drive. The officer tells him if he gets behind the wheel, he will be arrested. The debate only ends as the officer reaches for his handcuffs and the man hands over his keys. They have obviously been through this before. As the man begins his walk home, the officer watches and shakes his head, conflicted as to whether to arrest him or let him go. The threat of filling out paperwork turns the tide in the man's favor, and the officer drives away in the opposite direction.

His efforts to navigate home are almost comical in nature. From across the street, I tail him, and must hold back my laughter at times. Occasionally, the effects of his drinking cause him to lean against trees and fences, to keep his balance. He stumbles and lands on a garbage can. He rolls in its spilled contents, as he attempts to get up. Dogs bark from a backyard and a porch light turns on. "Get your ass out of here, you damn drunk!" a man shouts out from a partially open door. "Fuck you! C'mon out, you coward. I'll make you eat those fuckin' words," is replied. No one arrives to take the challenge. Instead, the light is turned off and the exaggerated sound of a deadbolt latching is heard. Mumbling obscenities, my pathetic target continues.

This man serves no viable purpose. I imagine his wife, only a few blocks away. She is dreading his entrance to their home, and fearing the attack she will endure in his drunken stupor. How her life has changed from the love they once had, and the commitments they'd made to each other. His attacks are growing more and more intense, and the bruises more common. She is tired of wearing extra make-up, sunglasses, and long-sleeved blouses to the grocery store, to cover them from the prying eyes of others. They hinder her attendance at school functions for her children, for fear of creating suspicions of abuse in the home. She could not bear to lose them to social services. Sadly, she has stopped praying to God for assistance. He has only proven himself to be one who ignores her words and turns his back on her suffering, and that of her children. Death is her only answer, but it is a step she cannot take. She must survive to do her best in protecting her children.

Without her acting as a buffer, they would stand no chance. She is trapped.

I cannot allow her to stay that way.

My target stops and unzips his fly. Exposing himself, he seems to be trying to write something on the pavement as he relieves himself. He seems amused and chuckles loudly. As he finishes and fumbles to zip his pants, he turns and begins to stumble, once again. I break into a run and cross the street. I stay in the grass, between the street and the sidewalk, and increase my speed. I bring up my arms into a lineman's stance and hit his shoulder blades with all my weight. He flies forward and lands face-down, his head bouncing against the concrete walk. I aim between his legs and kick, repeating it two more times. He hunches up in pain, but my foot again shoves him forward. I drop my weight heavily upon his back and hear his gasps to draw air back into his body. My hands grab the sides of his head and I slam his face into the concrete until all resistance and consciousness is eliminated. He is now mine.

I roll his limp body into a yard, partially hiding it from the street, by a hedge. I stuff his mouth full of napkins from a fast food restaurant, and wrap duct tape around his head to secure their placement. With some of the windows open in the surrounding houses, any noise has a chance of being heard. It is a weakness in my planning, but allows me to complete the act, without having to load him in a vehicle and drive him somewhere to do so. I learned in the beginning one cannot overestimate their abilities or strength, and have remembered never to do so. Next, I use the duct tape to bind his arms and legs. My breathing is accelerated and adrenaline flowing, as I inspect my work. I have done well. The voices will praise me later.

Sitting on his chest, I open a vial of smelling salts and hold them below his nostrils. He awakens and begins to struggle with his bonds. His muffled voice sounds from behind the duct tape, louder than I'd anticipated. I hold my knife to his throat and threaten him with death, if he continues. A minor jab of its point helps him to understand, and silence returns to the neighborhood.

"Now, listen and listen good," I whisper, with authority. "I know you are intoxicated, so you won't understand everything I say. I will try to make it simple. You need to know why this is taking place."

His eyes bulge and an expression of hate and fear combine. I know he wants to kill me—it is his way of dealing with life. I know not where his tendencies for violence were birthed, but I do know where they will die.

"You are a waste of a human being. The violence you use upon others is now being returned. The bruises you've inflicted, the tears you've brought, and the mental scars you've ingrained into innocent minds are at an end. There is nothing you can say or do to stop the process demanded by the voices I hear. Your chances to change your behavior are over, as is the life you knew. As it is demanded, it will be done."

It was then he realized he was going to die. His eyes began to glisten as the tears began to appear. The whimpering behind the tape seemed as if he were asking for mercy—mercy he had never shown for any of those he'd abused. The voices sang out in my brain, "Here is the big, bad man showing his true side, one of fear. He begs for mercy from death, from pain, from revenge. Kill him!"

The steel blade held under his chin rammed deep into his throat. My skills ensured it sliced apart his vocal chords first, before continuing to open his windpipe to the night. I brought the blade down and cut his external jugular vein in two. I stared deep into his eyes, reflecting the streetlight above. I wanted to see them die, and know the brain behind them would no longer live to inflict pain.

His body ceased to move. The voices told me it was over and to leave. Yet, there was one thing left to do. I rolled over the dead body and dug out his wallet. Sticking it in my pocket, I rose to leave, just as a porch light from across the street illuminated. I took off running, hoping my hoodie would hide my face from anyone peeking out of their windows. Sirens wailed in the distance, and dogs began barking in response. At any sign of headlights approaching, I ducked down and hid behind bushes or parked cars, whichever was available.

Within minutes, I arrived at the home of my victim. Inside, his wife was waiting for her husband to return home. She still loved him, I'm sure, and the initial shock of learning of his murder would not be easy. Yet, as the insurance money came in, and the family no longer had to worry about being abused, life would be better for them. One does not look at the road along the way, only the destination. Perhaps the children would only remember the good times, and not the bad. If that be the case, in their father's footsteps they would not travel.

I walked to the front door and laid the wallet on the porch. Ringing the bell, I took flight and departed before it opened. It was my hope his wife would realize the deed had been done by one who cared, and not a street thug. The act would also confuse the authorities and, hopefully, direct their investigation to only those who knew the man. I'm sure their questions would find his death not worth devoting time better spent elsewhere.

There have been many to feel my blade, over the years. I once took an oath to heal and help those in need. There are times the only way to help is to listen to the directions of the voices. Their wisdom may include the need for a death to occur, in order to heal others. I will always listen to what they say.

There are those who would call me a psychopath. That is their right. Others might say I'm a modern-day vigilante. If I initiated my acts, I would agree. But it is the voices who drive them, not me. I will do so until they no longer demand my action, or my life is ended by another. I am here to serve, to end suffering, to do as I promised many years ago.

It is my life as a physician. It serves me well.

Think Positive

Whenever I get down and depressed, I remember the words of my grandmother, "It's not Christian to be all sad and mopey. Why wear a frown and scare people away, when you can wear a smile and make them happy to be around you?" When she passed away and laid in a coffin, I remember her face had a slight smile. It took away my tears and brought a smile to mine, as well. I later learned it to be her natural smile, not one manufactured by the morticians. Her words made sense to me, upon that discovery. It is the duty of a Christian to cast off the negatives of life, and from the Devil, and be happy. It was then I decided I needed to live my life the same way.

For decades, I lived my life according to her words. I found a wife who accepted my philosophy, and we attempted to raise our children the same way. I understand your apprehension in listening to what I have to say. There are many Christians, as well as those who exude positivity, who can drive you crazy with their endless banter. Most individuals look at them as if they're completely insane, and hate it when they begin to "preach" at them. I made a habit of not pushing my religion on others. Instead, I figured leading by example was the way to inspire. If others asked how I could always look at the bright side of things, I would tell them. Otherwise, I just let my actions speak for me.

Doing this wasn't always easy, especially at my place of employment. I was a manager for a sales organization, and worked for a boss who believed degrading his employees was the way to get the most out of them. Whenever he wanted a raise, he would cut the commissions paid to his sales force, or benefit packages for all employees. This made things difficult for all managers to maintain a positive organization. I found myself telling my crew, "This is an opportunity for you to learn how to work smarter, not harder. Show him you can still make the paychecks you're accustomed to, instead of letting it get to you."

Work wasn't the only place my beliefs and practices were challenged. Most of the time, I was able to discover some way of looking at a tragedy and making it a positive. We'd lived next to an elderly widow for years, whose life was ended by a heart attack one August afternoon. The wife and kids had grown close to her, and the loss hit them hard. After the funeral, the tears were flowing. I gathered them in the living room and said, "Hey, don't be sad … be happy! For one, she's never going to be in pain again. Nor will she ever be lonely. Her spirit can join that of her husband. And, what's even better than anything else, together their spirits can travel all over the world and see the sights they always wanted to see. They can see the pyramids, the Taj Mahal, and even the top of Mt. Everest. They're not hindered by age or pains, they're free to soar the skies and see all they desire."

Sometimes it helps, sometimes it doesn't.

Not long after, we were spending a night at home, as all families should. The boys were on their notebooks doing homework, the wife was reading a romance novel, and I was watching a ballgame on television. Outside, a major storm flashed its lightning and roared its thunder, as the downpour flooded the streets. I did a quick channel check and was slightly disappointed there wasn't a good horror movie scheduled. It was a shame to waste such a wonderful storm without one.

Between the rumbles of thunder, we began to hear what sounded like an oncoming locomotive. Living in Tornado Alley, we realized our worst nightmare was about to be a reality. Rushing to the basement for shelter, we huddled together in one corner. To alleviate fear, we discussed all the new things we could purchase with the insurance money we would receive, after the tornado took our old ones. Of course, we would lose everything we had, but thinking about all the new stuff made all of us feel much better.

It was better than all of us freaking out and crapping our pants.

The wife and boys played along better than I imagined they would. That is, until the twisting of the house began. The creaks and groans of the upper level as it strained, and the popping of the home's major supports snapping, helped us to decide it was time for praying. We had little fear, as we knew God would protect his flock. Yet, we also knew God's plans didn't always coincide with our own. If I said we weren't a bit nervous, I'd be lying.

Fully caught in the force of the funnel, the roaring of the fierce wind did little to drown out the banging and thumping of our possessions, as they were slammed from one wall to the next. The unequal pressure of the basement to that of the upstairs, rattled the stairway door and ripped it from its hinges. Holding onto each other, I screamed, "Keep your faith. God will protect us!"

As the wall above us swayed, and then tore from its supports, I hoped my words would hold true.

Drywall and wooden frame studs burst into pieces and shot through the air. I wrapped my arms around my family, and did my best to use my body as a shield to protect them. Unspeakable pain engulfed me as dozens of splinters pierced my back and neck. I did my best to hold onto them, until the adjoining wall did the same, sending another surge my direction. My head was rammed forward as my skull was penetrated, and I began to lose consciousness. I was spinning in the darkness, hearing only the screams of my wife and children. I did my best to rise and present an impenetrable barrier to any more missiles, but failed. Instead, I felt the wind pulling me away, and slamming me against the concrete blocks across the room, before passing out.

I woke in a hospital, the television on the wall broadcasting some midday soap opera. A young woman was sticking an intravenous needle into my hand. She smiled upon seeing my open eyes. "Well, good morning to you. It's good to see you finally waking up. I'll get the doctor and be right back."

Wondering how long I'd been unconscious, I became aware of the constant throbbing in my head. I realized I was in a hospital, but had no idea where my family was. I needed answers, not only to where they were, but how were they? Had they been injured? Where were they living? Was the church taking care of them?

The nurse returned and said the doctor would be with me in a few minutes. I asked her the questions ricocheting around my brain, but all she kept telling me was to relax and not worry ... that I needed to concern myself with getting better, and only that. Frustrated, I lay back and prayed for their well-being. I knew God had protected them, and they were safe. They had to be.

My mouth felt like it was filled with cotton. The pitcher of ice water, sitting on the tray table next to the bed, looked so tempting. I tried to raise my hand to get some, but it wouldn't respond ... neither would the other. My legs refused to answer my requests to move, as well. I was paralyzed.

Another nurse entered the room and administered a shot, supposedly, to calm me down. Calm me down ... I couldn't move! What did they think I was going to do, riot in my bed? I chuckled at the thought. At least God was allowing me to keep my sense of humor. I was thankful for that.

I wasn't in much of a mood for the doctor's small talk. He avoided answering my questions as long as he could. Finally, he ran out of places to hide. "Mr. Dunkin, there is no easy way to tell you this. You were unconscious for almost a month. You are the only survivor from your household. Your wife and children were killed, and have already been buried. I'm sorry."

Every ounce of energy drained out of my body, in a matter of seconds. I was empty of all emotion. There would be no visits from my wife, no seeing the boys graduate from high school or college, no grandchildren to spoil rotten. The world I'd known was gone. God had allowed Mother Nature's fury to take it away. I wished she had taken me, instead.

My faith was being put to the test.

I immediately entered a state of deep depression. Over the following weeks, friends dropped by to see how I was doing, and to cheer me up. I admired the fact they tried, but the loss was much too great. To add to my misery, I still had several operations to make it through. As time progressed, all the wooden splinters were removed from around my spine, and feeling returned to my body. Within weeks, I was able to use my legs and arms once again. I should have been elated, but all I could imagine doing was visiting my family's graves.

As my release neared, I was provided more details of that fateful night. A very thin splinter had passed through my head, remarkably doing little damage. My family had also felt the sting of the flying missiles. With me being pulled away by the winds, they had sought shelter under the kitchen floor and the one remaining wall. Without the necessary supports, the floor had given way and dropped, crushing them. With the tornado hitting a major part of the city, there were hundreds injured, and locating them all took quite some time. It was hours before rescue workers arrived and heard the moans of my oldest son, the only one still alive. After suffering for so long, he died en route to the hospital. I was discovered only by one of the workers as he tripped over some debris and my feet appeared from under it.

Three months after the disaster, I was finally released. A golf buddy of mine (and my insurance agent) was kind enough to pick me up and drive me to my old homestead. He had already initiated clean-up processes, only the hole where the basement had been, and piles of debris, remained. Everything we had owned was gone.

Twenty yards away was the empty home of our passed neighbor lady. It had been virtually untouched by the tornado. I could see a few shingles missing from the roof, and the tree between her home and ours was uprooted and partially cut up by the work crews, but beyond that, the home had been missed.

It wasn't fair. How could God have chosen to have my family killed, all our possessions destroyed, and my life ruined … and allowed the empty home of the dead to survive? Was he so sadistic he found pleasure in seeing my grief? How could he be considered kind and merciful, when he let the innocent and children be killed? He wasn't anything my grandmother had thought him to be. He was a selfish bastard, who killed for his

244

own amusement—an asshole playing horrendous games with human lives.

The insurance company had temporarily set me up in a hotel until I could find appropriate lodging. I sat on the bed and stared at the dresser drawers in front of me. I had nothing to put in them. The only clothes I had were those I was wearing from the hospital's Lost and Found Department. I didn't even have a toothbrush. I laid back on the bed and cried, for the first time since my childhood.

During the next three days, I did nothing besides sleep, cry, and stare out the window at the normal families coming and going from the hotel. I didn't leave the room. There were no more prayers. God didn't answer them, so why ask him for anything? He didn't care.

Disregarding the Do Not Disturb sign on the door, a maid's endless knocking finally caused me to answer. "Hotel rules say I gotta come in and clean at least every three days," she shot at me, caring less about my mental state. "I gotta job to do. Gotta clean up. Might do you well to clean up, as well. You're getting mighty ripe, you are, mighty ripe."

Later that afternoon, another knock at the door interrupted my feeling sorry for myself. It was the friend who had brought me to the hotel, three days before. Setting down a couple of sandwiches, snacks, and cold drinks on the table, he gave me the lecture I needed to hear. "Look, I know you're hurting inside. I can't pretend to know what you're going through … and won't. But you can't go on like this forever. When you finish eating, I've got some forms for you to sign. One is some extra money from Disaster Assistance. It will help get you back on your feet until we settle your claim. Another is for a car rental I got you. It's sitting out front. You need to get out, go to the graveyard and pay your last respects, you know, bring some closure. The last one is a personal one. It's for five hundred dollars … a loan from me. Get yourself some clothes and go back to work. I was told your job is still waiting on you. You need to become normal again, get a schedule, something to take up your time, besides sitting here all depressed. People like you, and will help you. You just have to get off your ass and make the first move."

I almost choked on the sandwich I was stuffing into my mouth. Here was a friend, taking money out of his pocket, and going above and beyond, to help me get back on my feet. He was right, I had to start to live again. Tears coming to my eyes, I was on such an emotional roller coaster I could barely see the lines to sign upon.

"Oh, by the way, one more thing," he started before he walked out the door. "Remember this when it's time to renew your policies."

We both laughed as he left.

After a shower, I spent the afternoon shopping. I couldn't get the quality of clothes I'd had before, because of price. Regular shelf apparel from the department store would have to do. The folks at work would have to realize it takes time to build a proper wardrobe. I made sure to pick up the personal care items I needed, as well, especially the toothbrush. Car loaded, I drove a few blocks before deciding I was hungry again. I stopped for a quick bite at a fast food restaurant, and then headed out of town. On the outskirts, I stopped to pay my respects to my wife and kids in the cemetery.

It took a while to find their graves. I'd been hospitalized when they'd been buried, and had yet to select their monuments. I stopped at every grave marked only by the plastic name holders sticking up, until I found them. I was happy to finally locate them, but that emotion quickly changed. You cannot understand the emptiness that overwhelmed me. I stared at the green grass, knowing the bodies of my family lied six feet under, and envisioned their dead bodies lying in their caskets, slowly decomposing. My wife and I had been talking about having another child. I chuckled at how we'd make love after the boys had gone to sleep ... hoping they wouldn't wake.   Suddenly, my brain presented the image of me making love to her corpse.

I laughed. In its own way, it was funny to me.

Arriving at work the next morning, I found my friend hadn't been told the whole truth. In my absence, they had promoted another to my position. The owner offered me an entry-level position, as if he was doing me a favor. I showed my appreciation by loading up the boxes of personal items from my old desk they'd stored, and flipped him off as I departed.

My attitude had definitely changed.

My anger grew as I drove down the highway. I had always stood up for him. While his employees were having a hard time paying bills, he was flying all around the country, in his private jet, to college basketball games and rock concerts. He had even had the audacity to rub everyone's faces in it by posting pictures of himself at those events. Now, he was telling me to get lost. Before the tornado, I would've said, "Thank you for the opportunity of finding a better career elsewhere." Now, "Fuck you" sounded so much more appropriate.

I drove to the old homeplace, to gather my thoughts. There wasn't anything there, but simply being there felt somewhat comforting. It was as if I'd been drawn there for a reason. Contemplating my future, I had no idea what I was going to do. It wasn't that I was poor. The insurance money for the house would be in any day. It would more than pay off what was owed the bank, and would leave plenty for me to start over. But, did I want to?

The empty house next door drew my attention. It had sat vacant for months, and seemed to be calling out to me. My soul become heavy, as if I was being dragged down into a pit of bubbling tar. My vision blackened as it covered my eyes, and my lungs filled with the sticky goo. Intense heat seared my flesh, and the sound of it scorching filled my ears. I wanted to scream out, but found myself unable to do so.

Huge claws wrapped around my neck as I was pulled from the pit by a demon, and raised high, for others there to see. My angry thoughts of God's cruelty had been received, and accepted as a ticket for an interview. Was I sincere? Would I do anything to achieve the revenge I sought? Did I want such a God to have my soul, or would I rather one who understood my plight have it? Before I could answer, I was again dropped into the pit.

Coming to, I wasn't sure if I'd been in Hell, or only a nightmare. In front of me stood the bright yellow Real Estate sign. Suddenly, an idea came to me. Of course, every employee who has ever been fired wants revenge, but how many were willing to actually pursue it? I could succeed in doing so, and the answer sat right in front of me.

Two days later, I walked into that house. I'd persuaded the realtor to let me rent it for six months. They'd balked until I volunteered to keep it tidy, and available to show to potential buyers. As dusty and filled with mice as it had become during its vacancy, they understood the value my pitch presented. Although the old place wasn't home, my family was always close by.

For the first week, I did nothing but type out letters. I flooded the local paper, Better Business Bureau, and concerned government agencies with the illegal business practices of my old boss. Reporting false warranty claims, misreporting the number of hours employees worked to keep from having to pay overtime, and varying service costs from customer to customer were just a few of the violations reported. His misrepresentations to customers, employees, and regulatory agencies were listed, many times. State and Federal offices also received notification of his using his private jet for personal trips, but claiming them as business expenses on his taxes.

I signed the letters with names of various employees who'd received the similar treatment as I, knowing they would love to see the man go down. It wouldn't be the tirade of one, but the wrath of many, who had been wronged. The power of numbers would bring investigations.

My efforts bordered on obsessive behavior. I worked day and night. It was my mission in life, to see this man go down. God had screwed me over, and then my boss had done the same. I had plans for both.

Before I offered my soul to the devil angel, I wanted proof of his power. First, I called upon him to create frustration in the workplace. Chance of official investigations scared accountants. Illegal transactions and questionable items stopped being covered up. Products were destroyed, without visible culprits, in clear view of video cameras. Fires ignited in warehouses in the middle of the night, without due cause. Rumors began to spread, not only in the workplace, but all over the metro area.

The letters created interest, and audits by government agencies turned up inconsistencies and illicit business practices. Commissioned employees left in droves, as customers stopped purchasing from a company with a questionable reputation. Even banks began calling in their loans, afraid waiting any longer would only provide them with empty pockets.

Still, the owner acted oblivious to anything being wrong. His business was failing, but he was too egotistic to believe it wouldn't revert to its previous "successful" state. Instead of concentrating on business, his social media postings revolved around his annual hunting trip, private cabin, and new SUV. He was of the opinion his employees would feel good about working for a successful man, even if it was at their expense. To his employees, though, it was a slap in the face. Silver Spoon recipients, like himself, seldom achieved any level of greatness or respect close to that of their fathers. He was no exception.

He was doing just as I had planned.

The six months had passed quickly, and my lease term ended. I cleaned up the house, emptied the fridge, and took out the trash to satisfy our agreement. The few clothes and personal items I'd purchased were boxed up and packed in the back of an old pick-up truck I'd purchased. Before locking the door behind me for the last time, I took an envelope from my pocket and laid it atop the hall desk. It would be in full view, for the next arrival to read. Walking down the front steps, the

251

laughter of my dark acquaintances echoed from inside. They had been very helpful, up to this point. I would call upon them again.

Through our past conversations and social media postings, I had an excellent idea as to where the boss's cabin was located. I picked up a few supplies to get me through a day or two, and headed off. As the cabin lay less than fifty miles outside of the city, I made my way there (even after a couple of wrong turns) in a little over an hour. There it sat, empty of any occupant. I was pleased to see he had yet to arrive. My plan was working well.

I drove back down the dirt road, to a fire lane I'd seen on my way to the cabin. Backing in, out of sight, I began my waiting period. Never one to be punctual, I knew he would be along in a day or so. The interim gave me the time I needed to replay my future lines, over and over, until I could say it perfectly. Checking my cell phone, I found I had a weak signal, but that would suffice for the one phone call I would have to make.

Reflecting on the last several months, I dissected how the death of my family had changed me. Not only had I lost my positive attitude, but I had grown almost sinister in my activities. If asked, many would probably say I was taking out my anger at God's actions on one not deserving of such. Why would I, a Christian, ever consider inflicting pain on another? Perhaps, it was because of how much pain and suffering he had inflicted upon others, as well as my own. The man was worse than evil. He had no compassion for his fellow man. He was only concerned about himself ... no one else. He deserved everything coming to him.

Night in the wilderness arrived faster than expected. Wondering when my target would show, I amused myself, imagining visions of his facial expressions during the upcoming final climax. I cast off my impatience with the knowledge his supreme downfall was getting closer by the second. So was my future happiness.

As the morning sunlight peppered its way through the branches overhead, I woke and warmed up myself and the truck. I settled back with a couple of convenience store cinnamon rolls and a bottle of water, as the heater helped me shed the morning chill. It wouldn't be long, now. With the clear sky, it would be the perfect day to take pictures and brag on social media. I chuckled, in hopes it would be his last posting.

Around noon, his SUV whizzed by. I picked up my phone and made the call I'd planned. Within a couple of minutes, the script I'd imagined would come to be a reality. I gave him a few minutes to get his stuff inside the cabin, before heading off. Pulling up behind his vehicle, I parked and turned off my truck. Getting out, I touched the hood. It hadn't been driven far enough to warm it up and was still cool. That would work well with my plan.

"Hey," I shouted out. "Is there a little fat bastard anywhere around here?"

The cabin door had been open, probably allowing the fresh air in to replace the stale. Out stalked the one and only asshole I'd been seeking.

"Well, Mr. Dunkin, I presume," he replied, thinking he was reciting something amusing. "To what do I owe this pleasure? By the way, you do realize you're trespassing, don't you?"

"Don't matter much. I just thought it time you and I had it out, between us. I didn't much care for the way you put me out, after I'd stood by you all those years. Thought you should know that you're a sorry son-of-a-bitch that should live on a diet of dog turds and hog shit."

"Like I said, you're trespassing."

Keeping a smile off my face became a chore. This was more fun than I had ever imaged it would be. I could tell he didn't like anyone talking to him in that manner. If I kept it up, his ego would blow up. "You're lower than whale shit, and smell just as bad. This is the perfect place to beat the ever lovin' hell out of you. No witnesses. Just you and me. In fact, I think I'll do just that."

He froze as I took a couple of steps in his direction, with my fists clenched at my sides. It was easy to see the fear in his eyes. He was the one used to calling the shots. He felt himself superior to all, but he knew his limitations. Physical contact with one ready to beat the hell out of him wasn't in his repertoire. His next act was what I'd anticipated.

Reaching inside the doorway, he pulled a rifle and pointed it my direction. "Now, like I said, stay back. Don't make me shoot you. Get in your truck and drive off. You're already in trouble. I'm calling the cops as soon as you leave. You're going to end up in jail for as long as I can pay them to keep you. If you come any closer, I swear I'll shoot you in self-defense."

I didn't stop. I kept right on walking toward him, looking as menacing as I could. He gave me one more warning to stop, and when I didn't, fear got the best of him. He aimed and pulled the trigger.

The bullet tore into my chest and sent me backward, against the grill of his SUV. I was weakening but had to continue. "Shoot me, will you. You couldn't hurt me if you tried. Just for that, I'm going to wrap that fucking rifle around your neck."

I didn't have to take a step. I guess he figured he'd shot me once, so another time wouldn't matter. From the gurgling of the blood, I knew the second shot had ripped through my lungs. It was a definite kill shot … just as I had planned. Lying in the dirt, I kept telling myself, "Hang on, hang on, just a little longer."

I saw him the other day. He was still pissed at me for setting him up. I told him it was my pleasure, and moved on. I had things to do.

He's just one of many pissed at me. I kind of enjoy knowing that. It makes me feel more alive than I did when I was alive.

Yes, I had called the police that day, and pretended he had invited me up to the cabin to make amends but had really found out I'd written some of the letters to the newspaper, and wanted me dead. I'd even left a letter in the old house, expressing my apprehension at meeting him there, knowing he had found out what I'd done. I managed to stay alive just long enough after being shot for the police to arrive, and was able to whisper, "Why did it take so long for you to get here? You're too late. He shot me in cold blood. I don't even have a weapon."

His trial was a fast one. Even spreading money around, the evidence against him was much too strong. Seems calls to the police station were recorded. Jury found him guilty, and he was sentenced to life imprisonment. He didn't last too long in prison. Some inmate shanked him when he refused to be a good cell buddy and bend over, without a fight.

I kind of wandered around in Purgatory a while, after dying. Seems Heaven didn't want me because of my feelings expressed about God, and since I didn't sign any contract, I wasn't obligated to go to Hell. Having pissed them both off, I was a spirit without a home. One day, I happened upon my old neighbor lady and her husband. We talked a bit and she volunteered to help do what she could. Brought my wife down from Heaven. She's agreed to stay with me until God changes his mind and proves he can show a little mercy. She's positive he'll do so, sooner or later. Then, we can be with the boys, again, and be the family we once were.

Me? I'm no longer positive about anything. Actually, I don't give a damn. There's nothing like being a free spirit. Yep, the things I told my wife when she was mourning the old lady really do happen. I'm enjoying seeing the sights the wife and I never could afford to see. Fact is, we're on our way to Paris.

"Au revoir!"

The Hit

There was no change in how I received the job. The letter had been dropped through the mail slot in my front door. Just a blank envelope, no writing or stamp, but sealed. Inside, a picture and basic description of my target, his address, and a general schedule of his coming and going. The rest would be up to me.

Staring at the picture, I saw a familiar face. Probably not someone I knew personally, but his face was no stranger to me. Taking his information, I did a search online and found him to be a city commissioner. I guessed my employer had taken offense at some of the man's recent public statements, questioning the operation of the city, and its association with unions. He had pushed to weaken, and hopefully abolish, the labor groups. He was treading on dangerous ground. It was common knowledge the unions were money makers for organized crime. Mess around with the boys, and you'll find yourself pushing up daisies.

His days of permanently looking at flowers weren't far off.

I was surprised at the boldness of the organization. Making a statement was one thing, but doing so when attention had already been drawn to them was unusual. Normally, this person would be put aside until the attention was off him. Or a member of his family would be threatened to get him to shut up. Taking out a public figure was dangerous, not only to the one doing the job, but to those who would normally protect the boys. Judges, police investigators, even other politicians—all taking payoff money—would find their hands tied, with the public questioning anything that looked like it would protect the guilty. None of those liked having that type of spotlight shine on them. This would need to be a clean hit ... real clean. So clean no one could become a suspect.

Before choosing a method to eliminate him, I needed to have an idea where to do the job. I studied his schedule and researched everything I could about the places he normally visited. His routine was fairly well set. This made planning easier, but also made his security familiar with the places he visited, and the people who were employed at them. They would be aware of the danger spots ahead of time, and prepared for the surprises they might hold. This meant I would have to infiltrate a safe zone, where they might not expect one to attack.

I had my work cut out for me.

On Day Two, I followed the commissioner from a distance. His entourage included not only his vehicle, but one with four security personnel, following close by. Since there had been questions as to how the foes of his recent actions would react, a two motorcycle police escort preceded his car.

I had to laugh and cringe, at the same time. The son-of-a-bitch was getting more security than the mayor. My job wouldn't be an easy one.

There were places he stopped where I could have shot him. Problem was, they didn't provide a good getaway route. To use a sniper rifle, I needed to be on a rooftop, and high enough some bystander looking out a window couldn't see me from above. As hard as I searched, there were no places this could take place. Either I would have to be atop a skyscraper, shooting straight down at him, or take a chance on being spotted before I could get off a shot. Neither were attractive options.

I considered using a bomb, but with his office being in City Hall, and his home in a luxury apartment building, there was no guarantee I wouldn't kill a lot of innocent people. As bad as the organization wanted him dead, they knew the killing of innocents would end all political friendships and police force agreements. So that wouldn't work, either. In my research, I'd seen him to be one of the first recipients of an armored limousine. I'd have to blow up a whole street to ensure he'd die, if I set up a roadside device. So, no explosives.

Somehow, I was going to have to find a way to do the job. Since doing it from a distance wasn't going to be an option, getting up-close and personal would be the key. I just needed to find the door to unlock.

Getting home, I flipped on the television to give my mind a rest. I watched a comedy where the main character dressed up and got past a doorman. I started thinking, "Man, if it was only that easy. Wait a minute … what if it is?"

260

Day Three was devoted to figuring out how to get past the doorman, and into the luxury apartment building. To do so, I was going to need help ... at least one more person. I hated including a person who could later testify, if I were to be charged with the crime, but I needed a person with knowledge I couldn't gain in a day or two. I was halfway through my allotted time to get the job done, already, and couldn't waste a minute. I got on the phone, called up an old acquaintance, and invited him over. Within an hour, he showed up. Together, we lined up a plan I hoped would succeed.

Otherwise, I'd be the one pushing up the daisies.

The next morning, a Same-Day delivery package was place in a parcel box. The fee had been paid for online, with a stolen credit card, on a public computer, in the college library. There would be no way to trace where it had come from. I watched from across the street as the limousine pulled up and let the commissioner out. Through the front glass doors, I saw the security man hand him the package, along with other mail. Fifteen minutes later, I rushed to the building's front doors.

Facing the guard, I spoke with urgency. "We just got a call from some guy in Apartment C-76. He said he got a package with a snake in it. Luckily, he wasn't bitten. But, if you don't want the damn snake getting out of his place, and going into someone else's apartment, I need to get upstairs, fast!"

I'm not sure if it was the snake hook I carried with me, or the small cage, but the guard said, "Go", without hesitation.

"I need you to show me the way there," I added, acting as if I knew nothing about apartment buildings. "We can't waste any time. Hurry ... lead me!"

Riding the elevator, I hated to think about what was going to happen to him. I hated to kill an innocent, but security guards were almost expected to be killed. After all, they were nothing more than Rent-A-Cops, when it boiled down to it. I couldn't take a chance on him getting on the phone, if I went up alone, and alerting the commissioner to my arrival. After all, he hadn't called at all.

Exiting the elevator, I let the guard take the lead as we headed down the hall. Stopping at the right one, he knocked rapidly and shouted out the commissioner's name. I hoped he'd look through the peephole and recognize the guard. Within seconds, my wish was answered.

"Yes, Bert, what's all the banging about?"

I shoved "Bert" through the door with all my strength, knocking the commissioner back and onto the floor inside the apartment. As my reflexes went into action, I used my stiletto to slice the guard's throat, and kicked him backward, to avoid getting his blood on my clothes. The commissioner was doing his best to scurry away on his hands and knees, like a child trying to avoid a hated aunt's kisses. I jumped on his back and crushed his fat body down into the carpet, knocking the air out of him. I removed my favorite piano wire (with the leather hand grips on both ends) and ran it over the commissioner's head. Pulling it tight against the front of his neck, I leaned back and felt it cut deep into his throat.

"I'd use the knife on you, but the big boys want you to suffer a little. Hope you don't mind."

If he did, he didn't say a word.

Making sure both were dead, I did a quick search to find the package. I was surprised to find it open, and the commissioner having been so cool about things. Holding the ends, I popped it open and out dropped a neonate Black Mamba. I'd hoped that if I'd failed to get inside, the snake would take care of him. By the time anyone would have figured out what type of snake it was, he would have been dead. Trouble was, the shipping company hadn't handled the package with care. Somewhere along the route, the package had been crushed, along with the snake.

Knowing they can still bite by reflex, even when they're dead. I used the hook to place it in the cage I'd dropped upon entering the apartment. If anyone should see me leave, they'd have comfort in knowing the snake was dead, and not still loose in the building. My worries were unnecessary. I rode the elevator down alone, and walked out without any human contact.

Arriving home, I got rid of the snake down the garbage disposal and placed the hook and cage in the back of my car. I'd drop them off in some alley dumpster later. I disrobed, taking off the pads that added fifty pounds to my ass and stomach, before removing the fake beard and mustache. Finally, I took the gauze pads out from the inside of my cheeks. Any video taken would have the police looking for a much larger man. I'd never be suspected.

As common practice, I got online and went to a social media site. I navigated to one of the groups and messaged the site leader, "I want to be a member. So does a friend." When they received that message, they would know its meaning. In a few days, another blank envelope would be dropped in the mail slot. Only this time, it would contain my payment.

I turned on the scanner to listen in on the police calls. There was no indication of any murder taking place. I was a little surprised, especially since no guard would be on duty for any of the residents in the building. Surely, someone would report him missing. It was only a matter of time before the deaths were discovered. Tomorrow would be an interesting day for newspersons and police investigators. For me, I planned on taking life easy.

As I ate dinner, I thought back at how easy the kill had been. Using the guard to enter the apartment had been an epiphany. There would have been no other way. I couldn't wait for the commissioner inside, as I'm sure his alarm system would have picked me up. Pretending to be a common service technician wouldn't have worked, either. With cable and all other utilities running underground in the city, the guard would have been suspicious of anyone needing to be inside an apartment, instead of down a manhole. I had to come up with something the guard would believe, and be scared enough to allow himself to be used in such a manner. Luckily, ever since the hurricane, snakes have been a major problem in Miami. Bert had never doubted the emergency for a second.

Lying back in my bed, I listened to the ocean's waves crashing against the shoreline. I appreciated living in the outskirts of the city. True, I had to be aware of possible encounters with some dangerous wildlife, but as long as I stayed alert, I believed myself to be fairly safe.

The sounds of vehicle doors opening and shutting in the middle of the night brought me to the reality of there being more danger present than what the wildlife presented.

A major banging against my front door told me I had guests. Not having invited anyone who would use some sort of battering ram to gain entrance, I jumped up, grabbed a prepared briefcase and pistol, and headed down to the kitchen area. Sliding out the refrigerator, I entered a cubby and pulled the appliance back in its place. I knelt, opened a trap door, and slid under the house until I was behind the heavy hedge that surrounded the house. Peeking out, I saw a group of men in suits rush up the steps and disappear. Obviously, their battering ram had worked. Next time, I'd have to get a stronger door.

I took to the marsh, hoping I didn't step on a rattler or cottonmouth, in the darkness. When a log moved ahead of me, I jumped away and gave it a wide berth. Alligators don't like being stepped on, either. Entering a small outbuilding, I jumped in my extra sports car and sped off to new lands.

With no flashing lights, it was my guess my guests had nothing to do with the police department. No, they had probably been sent by my employer. He was paranoid, at times. Probably, he thought tonight's kill dangerous enough to have me killed, as well. That way, there would be no way the commissioner's assassin could talk, if caught. It was a smart move. Can't say I blame him.

Still, I did a job and he wasn't going to pay me. Add that to his attempt to end my life, and I get angry. I'll have to call my friend again. This time, I must remember to put Fragile on the outside of the package.

After all, we have to protect our little friends.

Feel Like Having A Cigarette?

"Man, you're going to love ghost hunting," the big guy hollered back over the front seat, as we headed deep into the woods. "I heard about this old house back here, that no one's ever been able to spend a whole night inside. Too many ghosts there to scare you away, they say. I'm excited as hell right now!"

I'd love to say his enthusiasm was contagious, but it wasn't. I had my doubts about anyone who said they'd seen or heard ghosts ... spirits of the dead ... paranormal sightings. Oh, I'd watched several of the shows on television, hyping up the time they spent chasing. Besides a few doors opening, or unexplained sounds in the homes, I had never seen anything but dust particles flying around the camera lenses, in the shots they'd shown. One might say I wasn't much of a believer, even though I wrote in the Horror genre for a living.

What? A writer of horror who doesn't believe? Yeah, you heard me right. I saw all the money some of the major writers were raking in and decided Horror was the genre that would pay the bills. Of course, a couple of my friends in the business told me that Erotica was the place to be, but writing all day and night about sexual experiences did nothing for me. No, having it and writing about it were two different things. Since my wife cut me off years ago, I'd have to rely on my memory, anyway, and that had seen better times.

What bothered me more than ghosts, was the group of guys I was with. Ray, the enthusiastic one, was a big sucker, six-foot-five and three-hundred pounds, minimum. No, he didn't carry his weight well, unless gathering it all in one place, atop his belt, was what that meant. I figure he'd given up dieting about the time he'd reached puberty, and that was about twenty years ago, at best. Jimmy was the exact opposite—kind of lean and mean, the quiet type. He didn't say much, so it was hard to gauge his education level, but since he was driving on a dirt path, his attention was diverted from our conversations. His jeans were of a more expensive brand, and his shoes were far from cheap, so I imagined he was either single and had money to spend, or had a substantial job somewhere. Bobby was Ray's son, and the spitting image of his father. One look told you they ate well at home, and could care less about maintaining an active lifestyle. I found myself biting my tongue, to keep from laughing, once or twice when he hit a rut and his fat belly jiggled so much, I could imagine it flying up and smacking him in the face. Yeah, like father, like son.

The SUV plodded through the weeds that had grown tall and thick, basically telling us we had no business traveling back into the boondocks late at night. My imagination created a scene, with a flat tire that couldn't be fixed because of all the rattlesnakes hiding in the weeds, just waiting for one of us to get out to try to fix it. Would serve all of us a lesson, if we really did get a flat.

Damn, a writer's imagination can be a terrible thing, especially in a place like this.

Although we'd only been bouncing around for five minutes or so, the density of the forest around us made me believe we had entered a forbidden zone. If there were such things as spirits and ghosts, this would be the ideal setting for them to reside, especially if they didn't want to be bothered by humans. Low hanging branches scraped the top of the vehicle at times, and various vines snagged the side mirrors and had to be pulled away. Again, I took it as a warning to stay away. I'd be leery of being in this area in the daylight, and here we were, here at night.

God, the stupidity I show at times boggles even my brain!

Another hundred feet or so passed under our tires before the headlights broke through the foliage and showed a clearing ahead. I heard the light sounds of some gravel popping out from under the wheels, as we made an immediate turn to the left. In front of us, the headlights illuminated our destination ... the old Bakerville home.

I recalled an Alfred Hitchcock movie and the house above the hotel, where a beautiful young woman was stabbed in a shower. This home resembled that one, only it was a little smaller, and needed a lot more attention. Exterior boards, long weather-stripped of any paint, hung loose in areas, as if they wanted to reach out and grab you as you walked by. The shutters, once operational, hung in pieces, as they'd rotted away over time. Windows had shards of glass remaining in most, but full panes were not to be seen. I guessed storms, swinging shutters, and vandals had taken care of most of them over time. No, this was not a place one would feel welcome visiting.

"Be it ever so humble," Ray whispered, before releasing an evil laugh. No one joined in his humor. This was not a place that had a "Welcome" sign hung for all to see. I figured the others were worried about the ghosts and spirits. Personally, I was more worried about the wildlife we might find, that had taken residency within its walls.

Jimmy parked close to the porch to make unloading easier. Ray and his son jumped out immediately and trod through the weeds to the back to begin the task. Jimmy turned back to me, with a worried expression on his face. "So, this is your first time. You picked the wrong place to start ghost hunting. I've heard some bad things about this place. If you start to freak out, I always keep a spare key in a magnetic tin box, under the driver's side front wheel well."

I nodded my understanding, not wanting to take a chance on my voice cracking with a verbal response. Scouting the area around the vehicle, I saw the forest had seemingly creeped our direction a few yards, since we had parked. Blinking, I shook my head to clear the brain and let out a slight chuckle. Perhaps ghost hunting and writing about ghosts had best be kept separate, in the future. It was clear my imagination was far too active.

Stepping into the weeds, I prayed I wasn't putting my foot down within striking distance of a copperhead—its venomous fangs shooting forward in attack. A twig brushed my calf and I jumped almost out of my shorts. Yeah, too damn much imagination.

I grabbed a box of oil lanterns and struggled to get them onto the porch. Common sense told me, if the stairs had been strong enough for both Ray and his son's weight, they would hold me, as well. Of course, there was always the scenario saying they had weakened them to the point of breaking under one more pound atop them, but the weight of the oil-filled glass lanterns told me to take a chance and hurry up them, before I dropped the entire box full. They had explained that since there was no electricity in the place, batteries would run out if we kept them going all night, and the oil lanterns would supply us the lighting we'd need. I'd worried about proper ventilation, but the broken panes of glass had eliminated that concern. So, dropping the box wasn't an option, unless I wanted to spend the evening in the dark. Guess what I thought of that?

Within a few minutes, the four of us had things set up. The lanterns did a fair job of lighting up the place, although the flames' flickering presented an eerie effect on the shadows, dancing against the walls. The handheld recorders were placed on the floor in the center of the room, for use in recording all the mysterious voices they'd planned on hearing over the evening. Ray's big expense, and pride and joy toy, had been his EMF (Electro Magnetic Field) detector. He made sure to keep it hanging around his neck, as if it were an alarm, of sorts, to paranormal presence. For his sake, I hope it worked for him.

We each chose a room and sat in silence for about an hour. I say, "Silence", but the sounds of Bobby and Ray's ripping open bags of chips and candy bars voided that completely. Finally, when they'd filled their stomachs, the house grew quiet. Now able to hear the sounds of the house, instead of crunching, the scurrying of tiny feet in the walls and ceiling gave proof the house had become a home to field mice. This, more than anything else, made me worry a bit. Since mice are food for snakes, it wouldn't be odd for the walls to hold several of them, as well. I flicked on my flashlight and scanned the floor, walls, and ceiling, just to ensure none had mistaken me for a large rodent.

Sitting cross-legged, with my back to a wall, I pulled out a cigarette and lit it. Immediately, Ray's voice rang out, "Hey, no smoking inside the house. I want to be able to smell any odor that may present itself, and cigarette smoke will ruin that. Go outside, if you're going to smoke."

Yeah, like the smell of the oil lanterns wouldn't cover up odors, as well. Going to the porch, I inhaled deep and wondered why in the hell I had come. This wasn't going to be anything but a bore over the next five or six hours.

It was only coming up on midnight, and already I was doing my best to keep my eyes open. If the seats in the SUV had been any more comfortable, I might have gone inside and asked Jimmy for the keys. My imagination ran wild, once more, and I giggled at a mental image of Ray listening to his recordings tomorrow and hearing only my snoring.

I stared into the darkness of the forest surrounding the house. There was no breeze, but the lower brush was moving, as if being pushed aside by some invisible force. I strained my eyes to see, and tuned in my hearing for the slightest sound, but nothing was there. Finishing my cigarette, I knocked off the hot ash and ground it into the rotting wood beneath my feet, before stuffing the butt into my jeans' pocket.

"Why did you do that?"

It was a female voice! I turned to my right, and there stood a young woman. I raised my flashlight to see her but felt her icy hand pushing mine back down, before I'd had a chance to even turn it on.

"Keep your light off," I was ordered. "Again, I ask thee, why did you do that?"

"What? Oh, you mean with the cigarette?" Her head, in the shadows, nodded. "It's what we did in the military. It's called field-stripping a cigarette. You put it in your pocket, to keep the grounds clean and free of trash. Plus, you don't have to pick it up later. Who are you?"

"So, you do it out of respect for my home?"

"I guess so," I responded, wondering if I was imagining the girl, or simply going mad. "I'm kind of anal about cleaning up after myself, and not making a mess for someone else to have to clean up."

"You have caring ways. Come with me." She took my hand and an icy chill flowed into my body. I was walking alongside her, but it felt as if we were floating atop the underbrush. I turned to glance back at the house, and saw multiple shadows entering the porch door and windows. The screams of those I'd left behind filled the darkness, and shots were fired, confirming my suspicions Ray had been armed. Cries of agony followed the girl and I as we drifted back the way I'd arrived, passing a dumping ground of rusting old cars and trucks, before reaching the main road. Together, we touched down on the pavement and stood staring at the other in the light of the half moon. She reached up, as if to pull my head down to her lips, but quickly pushed it away. "No, you deserve to live. Do not return to my home. None are welcome there."

And, she was gone. Yeah, she'd vanished, you know, like, into thin air.

It took me hours to get up the road. Oh, I stopped along the way several times, at houses, and knocked until my knuckles bled. Yet, no matter how hard I knocked, none would come to the door. Finally, about sunup, I found a farmer walking out to his barn to feed his livestock. Telling him my story, he told me to stay on his porch as he called the police.

Twenty minutes later, a couple of cruisers pulled into his place. Again, I told the story I'd already told once. Handcuffed, I was stuffed into the back of one of their cars and began the journey back to the place I'd been told to never return.

Arriving, the first thing I noticed was that the SUV was gone. Obviously, one or more of them had survived and driven home. Then it hit me. They hadn't passed me on the road. Where had they gone?

The officers entered the home, with their guns drawn. I didn't know if they were thinking I'd set a trap for them, or if they were going to meet up with something that their weapons would protect them from, but couldn't say much about it from the backseat in which I was being held. It didn't take long for them to return.

"Okay, what in the hell do you think you're trying to pull on us?" one of the officers spat in my direction. "Do you think it's a joke to pull us away from doing real police work?"

Okay, my imagination was active, but not that active. I'd not walked to the house all by myself. Surely there had to be some evidence of the others being attacked. "I don't know what you're talking about. When I left last night, there were all types of screams and such coming from inside. It took me forever to find someone to call you. People around here won't answer their doors at night."

The two shook their heads at each other, in disbelief and disgust. I learned there was nothing inside but several oil lanterns, still burning. No one or nothing else.

As we were leaving the property, I caught a glimpse of their SUV alongside some of the other vehicles, in the dump area. "Hey, there's their SUV! Stop, Officer, you've got to check it out."

The rest, I imagine, you've read about in the newspapers. Seems each of the vehicles in the dump had at least one skeleton in it—the SUV I'd pointed out had three. All had aged for a minimum of ten years, according to the examinations performed, even those in the SUV.

I guess the people living in the area had good reason not to answer their doors at night. Of course, the police scoffed at all the rumors and stories floating about, but I'd long learned that every rumor has a basis, somewhere. Luckily, I was released and sent on my way. Although forced to return once, I never did so again. I had become a believer.

There is a story to write about this event, yet, I know not where to begin. No one would believe me if I did, as my past reputation as a writer of horror precedes me. I think back to the girl refusing to kiss me. Did she do so to maintain her honor, or to keep from giving me the kiss of death? I'll never know.

I sit here, smoking my cigarette, and listen to my daughter preach to me about the dangers of smoking. I am tempted to tell her that smoking may not be as hazardous as one believes. In fact, there are times when smoking may save your life.

About the Authors

Richard C. Rumple spent years writing comedy for his radio show and stand-up comedy act, as well as training manuals as a Corporate Training Director, before he released his first novel in May 2017. "Horror Across the Alley" immediately received praise and positive reviews. His second, "They Lurk In Summer" hit the marketplace in August of the same year. It, too, has received great reviews. Intent on bettering his writing skills, he participated in a mentor program offered by the Horror Writers Association in early 2018, before starting his next book, a short story collection, "Gabriela: Tales from a Demon Cat." In addition, he has several short stories available in multiple author collections, is working to complete narration on his "Gabriela …" book for audio, and has a novella trilogy planned for completion the summer of 2019.

Charles Lynne is a writer and poet. He is a country boy who loves the outdoors. He claims that he could very easily live off the grid and disappear. He loves to read Stephen King books in his spare time. When he isn't writing, he is working on computers and various other electronics. Yet he still finds the time to keep his sister out of trouble, as well as finding ways to scare her. He enjoys working with other authors and learning new things to improve his craft. A few of the writers that have inspired him are Stephen King, Becky Narron, Sadie Whitecoat, Richard Rumple, Shaun Hupp, and Ray Garton.

Made in the USA
Middletown, DE
16 January 2023